Charla and the Rogue Watcher

Dianne Astle

Six Worlds Publishing
Hope, British Columbia

Dianne Astle/Six Worlds Publishing

This is a work of fiction. Names, characters, places, and
incidents are a product of the author's imagination.

Book Cover by Sean Sherstone **www.sherstone. com**

Charla and the Rogue Watcher/Dianne Astle. —1st ed.
ISBN 978-1-775226369

Other books in the series

Ben the Dragonborn 2013
Ben and the Watcher on Zargon 2015
Moses and the Dragonborn 2017

With thanks to the world's justice seekers and
peacemakers

1. Three Friends

He was only allowed to fly on dark moonless nights when there was less chance of being seen. Not that there were many people on the ocean to see him as the location was isolated, but an occasional boat would moor in the island's bays, and Miss Templeton believed in the adage that it was better to be safe than sorry.

On this night the dragon, whose name was Ben, carried his best friend Denzel Carter and a girl he loved who did not love him back. Allison said he was like the brother she never had, which were words Ben did not appreciate hearing.

Ben landed on a high point of land overlooking the ocean. As soon as Denzel and Allison climbed off his back, he transformed from a dragon into a teenage boy with brilliant green eyes. The three friends each found a rock to sit on and stared out at the ocean.

"It would be nice to fly up here in the daytime, so there was more chance of seeing whales," Allison said.

"Anytime I see an orca, it reminds me of riding through the waves on the back of a creature very much like them on Lushaka," Ben said. "I'd love to go back there now that I'm not terrified of being in water over my head."

"I'd love to go there someday and meet Charla for myself," Denzel said.

Ben picked up a rock and threw it into the ocean. "She's a character," he said. "I never dreamed I'd meet a mermaid or that when I did, she'd be so annoying."

"From what you've told us, she saved your life several times," Allison pointed out.

"Yes, she did," Ben agreed.

"Do you think they're treating the brownies any better on Zargon?" Allison asked.

"They'd better be," Ben said, remembering the time when the three friends were together on a quest to save his grandfather. "Or else, there won't be any brownies left on Zargon, they will all be on Farne."

"Have you heard how things are going on either of those worlds?" Allison asked.

"No," Ben replied.

"You guys are so lucky," Denzel threw a rock he'd been holding. "I've only gone to one world, and I'm beginning to think I'll never go anywhere else again. I saw Miss Templeton last week, she tested me, and the dials of her Medallion just spun around and around without stopping anywhere."

"That means you're going somewhere, sometime, but who knows when and where," Ben said.

"I guess I should count myself lucky to know about the school's true purpose otherwise I wouldn't have any chance of going off-world," Denzel said. "Have either of you been to see Miss Templeton lately?"

Allison shook her head, then said no as she realized Ben and Denzel couldn't see her in the dark. "But Trevor was tested last week, and he's going off-world soon."

Ben felt the familiar burning pain in his gut at the mention of Allison's on-again-off-again boyfriend. He was glad it was dark, so she wouldn't see the wisp of smoke escaping from his nostrils. That had been happening a lot lately. If he didn't find a way to prevent it, someone who didn't know his secret was going to notice.

"What world and when?" Denzel asked.

"Mellish, in ten days," Allison said.

"How did he get to be so lucky?" Denzel asked. "He's been off-world more times than anyone else at the school. I hope the dials point to what world I'll go to soon. I don't care where I go, I just want to go somewhere."

Most students were still waiting to go on their first off-world mission as companions to adult alumni. Ben was an exception. So were Allison, Denzel, and Trevor. They had all gone off-world without the supervision of an adult.

Ben sat on his rock in shocked silence.

"How about you, Ben?" Allison asked. "Have you been tested lately?"

"I was today," Ben stammered.

"Why didn't you tell me?" Denzel asked.

"You were so disappointed not to be going somewhere yourself, I found it hard to tell you. Believe me when I say I wish it was you going instead of me."

"Okay, so where are you going?" Denzel asked.

"It appears Trevor and I are going to Mellish at the same time." When Ben said the name Trevor, he couldn't keep the sneer out of his voice or sparks from coming out of his mouth. When he finished speaking, there was not only smoke but flame.

"This is not good," Denzel said.

"Ben, you need to get over your unreasonable dislike of Trevor," Allison said. "Especially if you are going off-world together. The Guardian of the Six Worlds has a good reason for choosing the two of you, but you'll sabotage the mission if you can't work with Trevor."

If Allison hoped to help Ben see things in a different light, she failed. The smoke and flame increased as she spoke. When she stopped talking, Ben sat in silence for a minute as he took a few deep, calming breaths.

"I hope the three of us will go together again sometime," Ben said when he was more composed. "I like having friends I can trust by my side." Ben's words were the wrong ones if he wanted to stay calm. The smoke that had almost died down came back. Allison coughed when some of it got in her face.

"I'm not sure if I'll ever go off-world again," Allison said when she stopped coughing. "Healers usually stay home unless they are sent to another world to train someone else in the art of healing." Allison stood up from the rock she was sitting on. "It's getting late. We should head back."

Ben stood and transformed back into a dragon, then crouched down to make it easier for his two friends to climb onto his back.

"Could we go further north and see what's happening on the next island?" Denzel asked.

"I think we should go back. Tomorrow is a challenging day." Allison climbed onto Ben's back. "Actually, we have two challenging days ahead of us. I don't understand why they think it's a good idea for us to stay overnight underground."

"I agree with Allison. We should head back," Ben said in his gravelly dragon voice.

As Ben flew back to Fairhaven, he thought about Mellish. He had studied all five worlds Earth was linked to in the special library open to students who knew the school's true purpose. Ben knew that Mellish was a small world, and the only part of it inhabited was in what he would think of as the North. The sun was too hot on most of the world to allow for human habitation.

There were five cities and several small towns. The capital was Nortown. At the heart of this city was a palace where the ruler lived. Outside Nortown was a fortress where the Watcher of the world was supposed to live. Only the current Watcher had rebelled against the Guardian of the Six Worlds and moved into the palace three years ago. Some of that world's Chosen had joined him. Since Grek had seized political power, he had stolen land and resources from the people of Mellish. Several Chosen had refused to join Grek as world rulers and had become part of an emerging Resistance instead. The promise of wealth was not enough for them to betray the Guardian.

The following morning, when Ben arrived late to the dining hall, he looked for Allison and saw her sitting with Trevor. Trevor was the most popular student at the school. He was particularly admired by those who knew the school's true purpose. He had been off-world five times.

Ben had been off-world three times himself, but most students only knew about his last trip, when he had gone with Denzel and Allison to help rescue the King of Zargon. And even then, the students had not been told the whole story. They didn't know he'd gone to that world as a Dragonborn, and the King they rescued was his grandfather.

Ben felt his stomach burn when he noticed Trevor and Allison holding hands underneath the table. He tried to push his jealousy aside, but couldn't do it. He wished one of the teachers would come and put a stop to it, but none of them seemed to notice. If they did they had decided to ignore the romance.

The school discouraged students from getting romantically involved with one another, but it was hard to stop romance when teenagers were together for a long time. Ben had interrupted more than one couple kissing in the far corners of the library, and more than once heard giggling from the loft in the barn. So far, he hadn't stumbled into Allison and Trevor, which was a good thing as he wasn't sure he could keep his dragon reactions in check.

He was staring at Allison and Trevor when Denzel jabbed him in the ribs with his elbow. "What?" he said, turning to look at his friend.

"Where there's smoke, there's fire," Denzel said.

Ben looked up to notice a small cloud of smoke hanging just over his head. At the table next to theirs, a grade nine student was staring at him with a quizzical look on his face.

"Thank you," Ben mumbled. He turned away, so Trevor and Allison were not in his line of sight and took a large drink of cold water. He was grateful Trevor was not in the same grade as he and Allison. It would be unbearable to watch them together all day in the classes they shared. The school had fewer than one hundred students scattered between grades nine and twelve so there was no escape from someone in the same grade you were in. As that thought crossed his mind, a second thought horrified Ben. What if Allison was tested in the next few days and ended up going to Mellish with him and Trevor? Ben couldn't think of anything worse. He couldn't bear the thought of working closely with the two of them on another world.

2. At School

Ben groaned when he discovered that Mr. Smith, a teacher with an eye patch and a hook, was to be their substitute math teacher. His presence meant their regular teacher was off-world again. It was one of the things he and Denzel had first noticed about Fairhaven. The teachers were away a lot, leaving them in the care of substitutes.

Mr. Smith was seriously wounded on a trip off-world. Not for the first time, Ben wondered if they kept him on as a substitute because he reminded the Chosen to be careful as the missions they went on were not without risk.

"Miss Suzuki is on Zargon," Mr. Smith said. "I will be your teacher until she comes back."

Ben wasn't the only student suppressing a groan. Mr. Smith was a crusty man with little patience for students who didn't pay attention one hundred percent of the time. He wanted them sitting at their desks and ready to work five minutes before class began. There was no grace offered to those who were late. He walked around with a ruler that had slapped Ben's desk more than once.

Then the full impact of Mr. Smith's words hit him. He had just told the entire class where Miss Suzuki had gone.

He had never heard a teacher say something like that before. In grades nine and ten, not every student had known about the school's true purpose, and the principal and teachers had stressed that the students who did know had to keep it a secret.

Ben realized that all the students in grade eleven must now know that Fairhaven trained the Chosen of the Guardian. Of the two students who hadn't known by the end of grade ten, one hadn't returned to Fairhaven for grade eleven, and the other had recently learned about their role in helping the Guardian seek justice and protect peace on other worlds. Ben felt a momentary sadness for the ones who had left the school and a deep sense of gratitude that he wasn't one of them. It had looked like he might not be staying at the school in grade nine, but when Miss Templeton tested him, he had immediately gone through a portal to another world.

By mid-afternoon, the class was on the beach, holding windsurfing boards. Phil Tanner, the Physical Education teacher, and Mr. Smith were just off-shore in a sixteen-foot aluminum boat that carried a backpack for each one of the students.

Ben noticed Trevor was near the boat with a windsurfing board of his own. Ben wondered what he was doing there.

"I've asked Trevor to come with us today because he made this trip look easy last year. He is an excellent mountain climber," Tanner said.

Ben ground his teeth. He had been hoping for some time alone with Allison.

"Many of you will find it challenging," Tanner continued. "Instead of climbing the outside of a mountain, we will be climbing inside the mountain in the dark."

"Cool," Denzel said. "I'm going to enjoy this." It took a lot to satisfy Denzel's thirst for excitement. On the other hand, Ben would prefer not to climb in the dark, either on the inside or the outside of a mountain.

When they got on the water, Denzel was way out in front of the class. Like Trevor, he excelled at this and all other required sports. Ben guessed he would be the helper with next year's class.

Ben trailed behind to keep an eye on Allison and help her if she fell off her board, but it wasn't Allison who fell off. Ben didn't know what hit him. One moment he was riding the waves, and the next, he was under them. The old panic Ben felt when his head was underwater overcame him for a moment, and he thrashed his arms and legs. He bobbed to the surface at an inopportune time. A larger than usual wave picked up the windsurfing board and smashed it down on his head. Trevor came by when Ben was in shock from the pain and asked if he wanted help.

"No," Ben said emphatically as he pulled himself on top of his board and lay across it. Trevor disappeared out of sight, and Ben floated alone.

Phil Tanner motored over to him. "Ben, are you all right?" he asked.

"Of course, he is," Mr. Smith said. "Any kid that's been off-world three times can survive a fall off a windsurfing board."

Ben didn't feel all right. He had swallowed some saltwater and his head hurt. He lay face down on the board, waiting for the coughing to stop so he could try to stand. Ben discovered he was dizzy when he did try, and it was impossible to remain upright on his board. He fell into the water, pulled himself back onto it, and tried to stand again, but his knees were still too weak.

"Take it easy. We're almost there. We'll tow you the rest of the way," Tanner said as he came alongside Ben and connected the board to the boat.

The windsurfing boards of all the other students were onshore when Ben arrived. He crawled off his board and dragged it onto the sand before flopping down beside a log. Denzel picked up Ben's board and carried it further up shore where no rogue wave could take it away. A hand touched Ben's shoulder, and he knew without opening his eyes that it was Allison. "Are you okay," she asked.

Ben made a feeble attempt at a joke. "I don't know what I ever did to that board, but it doesn't like me."

"It looks like a goose egg is forming on your forehead," Allison said.

Ben reached up and touched the place where the board had hit him. Allison was right. She pushed his hand away, then gently covered the goose egg. He felt heat radiate from her hand and flow into his head.

"Don't use too much of your energy," Ben said. "You may need it, and it won't hurt me to have a bump on my head."

Allison ignored him and continued to send her healing power into him. When she finished, Ben's head no longer hurt. He touched the place where the goose egg had been to discover it was gone. Not only that, but he felt full of energy. He felt better than he had for a long time.

"Thank you," Ben said to Allison, then he stood and looked around to see what the other students were doing. Denzel was halfway up a rope that hung from a large tree growing on the mountainside above the mouth of the cave. On his head was a helmet with a light attached to it, and his backpack was over his shoulders.

Students who had their backpacks were waiting in line to climb the rope. By the time Ben and Allison got to the boat, theirs were the only backpacks that remained in it. Ben knew each bag contained similar things: runners, a change of clothes, a cup and a spoon, a space blanket and a mat, a day's worth of food, and a straw that could filter impurities out of water.

Mr. Tanner had already climbed the rope and was at the mouth of the cave Denzel was trying to reach. The physical education teacher would accompany them into the mountain, while Mr. Smith stayed on the beach overnight to ensure their windsurfing boards were safe from theft. Although the area was remote, theft still happened once in a while.

Ben put on a helmet and stood beside Allison. Trevor was holding the rope steady for the students climbing it. Allison climbed first and then Ben followed her.

"It's time to put the rock climbing we've been teaching you to use," Tanner said when they were all inside the cave. He turned and climbed a rock wall until he was at a spot just above their heads. "You've done everything we'll ask you to do before. The only difference is you're doing it inside a mountain rather than outside of it. The important thing is not to panic. There are imperfections on the wall in front of you that you may not be able to see, but you can feel them. If you need any help, Trevor will give it."

"Let's go," Denzel said to Ben.

"I'm going to wait and see if Allison needs help. She drained some of her power away by healing me."

Allison gave him a dirty look. Even in the semi-dark, Ben could see it. She had clearly heard him. She moved closer to him so she could speak without the others hearing. "Ben, for crying out loud, stop worrying about me. I have more than enough energy to do this. Not only that, but if I run into trouble, Trevor is here to help me. It's his job, not yours. What's going on with you, anyway? You've been way over the top lately."

Ben didn't say anything as he watched Denzel and then Allison climb the cave wall.

"Okay, Ben," Trevor said. "It's your turn. When you get up there, leave my girlfriend alone."

Ben felt heat rise from deep within. He battled to push it down. If he gave Trevor a life-threatening burn, Allison would never forgive him. Thinking about Allison's reaction was what finally put the fire out.

3. Inside the Mountain

As the class moved through the tunnels, Allison couldn't

help but wonder what kinds of bugs lived here. There didn't

seem to be spiders, but the people in front of her might be
clearing the webs away. The thought made her shudder.
She wondered where the bats were. Surely, there must be

bats. Weren't there always bats in caves?

There were places where they had to take their
backpacks off and push them in front of themselves as they
crawled through the tunnel on their bellies. At other times
they moved along a ledge on the side of a rock wall with no
idea how high above the floor of the cave they were.
Allison wished the lantern on her helmet was brighter so
she could see the ground. An image of the bones of
previous students who had fallen off the ledge flashed
through her mind. She pushed it aside by telling herself the
school would never bring them here if it were as dangerous
as it felt. They spent the majority of the morning climbing
upward as they moved through the dark. Eventually, the
narrow tunnel opened up into a cavern where a small
waterfall trickled down from somewhere above them.

"This is where we will eat our lunch. The water is safe to

drink." Tanner leaned into the water and took a drink. Most
of the students followed his example and drank directly
from the waterfall, but Allison and a couple of other

students took out the cups they carried in their backpacks and put them under the flow of water, then drank through the straw which removed impurities.

"So far, it's been easy going," Tanner said. "But it's about to get more difficult."

Allison stopped breathing for a moment. The whole experience of rock climbing in the dark had not felt at all easy to her. She was sure most of the other students would agree.

"The next step is more challenging because we need to lower ourselves down a chimney cave," Tanner continued. "There will be a rock wall to rappel off for about one hundred and twenty feet. After that, there is approximately another twenty feet of open space. Be ready for it and don't panic. You will wear a safety harness, and we can lower you down if necessary, but I'd prefer you use the rope to lower yourself down as we taught you to do on the bluffs near the school. You likely won't have a harness when you go off-world and need to go down the side of a cliff or a building, so you need to become confident rappelling without one. Trevor will go first and will be at the bottom to help you. I will go last. The chimney cave is this way."

Tanner walked past Allison toward the far side of the cavern.

Allison shuddered when she thought of the day when they were taught how to rappel using only a long rope thrown around a tree. They had put one end of the rope around their waists and the other end between their legs. She was warned to wear thick clothing but still ended up with a burn where the rope rubbed against her side. Her hands had a red mark across them from trying to keep the rope from slipping through the knot too fast. It had been one of her least favorite days at Fairhaven. She hadn't tried doing it again even though they had been encouraged to keep practicing. She'd told herself that as a healer, she was unlikely to go off-world again anyway. She was sure it was something she did not need to know. Now she wished she'd practiced.

"Stay close to the side of the cave," Tanner said. "There are holes in the cave floor; if you step in one, I have no idea where you will end up." He led them downstream away from the waterfall past a place where the water disappeared through a hole in the ground. They gathered around a large hole in the cave floor.

Allison waited until the only students who remained near the waterfall were herself, Ben, and Trevor. Ben showed no sign of moving, and she knew Trevor felt his place was at the back of the line. Once more, Allison felt irritated by Ben's obsessive desire to protect her. She would have liked some time alone with Trevor. She stepped closer to him and kissed him on the lips knowing Ben would be able to see them by the light from his helmet. There was smoke in the air when she turned and walked toward the chimney cave.

Trevor stayed where he was for a few moments with a quizzical look on his face.

"Remain where you are until I call your name," Tanner

instructed. "Trevor."

Trevor slipped past the rest of the students until he was at the front of the line. Once there, he was clipped into the safety harness attached to ropes anchored in rock. Then Trevor was given the ends of another rope, which connected to a second anchor point. Trevor wrapped the rope around himself as they were taught. He took hold of the second rope and stepped backward into the chimney cave. Trevor made it look effortless. The students listened in silence to the sound of his feet pushing off against the side of the cave as he rapidly lowered himself down.

Allison grew more anxious. She expected her name to be called next. She reasoned that Mr. Tanner would want a healer at the bottom in case someone was hurt on the way down. She let out a relieved breath when the next name was

not hers, but Ben's.

Allison could see the worry in his eyes from the light on her helmet as Ben passed by. She knew his concern was not for himself, but for her. For the first time that day, Allison grudgingly acknowledged that he had reason to worry. She was frightened and wondered if her fear would prevent her from successfully descending the rope.

It crossed her mind to refuse to rappel into the chimney cave, but then what would she do? She couldn't find her way back on her own, and she wouldn't want to sit alone in the dark waiting for the others to return.

As she guessed, Mr. Tanner did want a healer at the bottom. Her name was called after Ben's. Her legs felt weak, and she might have stumbled right into the cave opening if Denzel hadn't jumped forward and grabbed her.

He took her arm and walked forward with her. He helped take her backpack off. The plan was to lower the packs down the tunnel separate from the students. Tanner clipped her into the harness, and Denzel helped her position the rope she would use for rappelling.

"Walk backward into the hole," Mr. Tanner instructed.

Allison stood frozen in place. Her feet just did not want to move. Denzel took her arm and turned her around so her back was facing the mouth of the cave. He put her hands in the proper position on the rope and stood in front of her with his hand on her arm.

"Come on, Allison, you can do this," Denzel whispered. "You have a safety harness on. You're not going to fall. If you can't rappel for some reason, we'll lower you to the ground."

Allison hesitated for a moment and then gathered every scrap of courage she possessed and took a short step backward. There was still solid rock under her feet. She took another step and balanced on her toes at the edge of the chimney cave. She didn't choose to take the last step backward but lost her balance and slipped. She couldn't stop herself from screaming. She was overwhelmed by panic as she swung back and forth over the cave opening, held in place by the harness. With effort, she cut the scream short. She gasped for air and tried to take some deep, calming breaths as she hung half in and half out of the cave.

"Try again, Allison," Tanner said. "I've taught you how to do this. Just remember to keep your legs perpendicular to the wall and your body leaning in toward your feet as they walk you down. Hold on tight, and let just a bit of rope out at a time, and you'll do fine."

Allison's hands were shaking. She let out too much rope, and the lights on the other student's helmets disappeared as she dropped into the hole. She swung around in circles in a panic. Denzel lay down on the ground, so his head and arms were over the side of the cave. He reached out and stopped the wild twisting of the rope and stabilized it, so she was in the position she needed to be in to start her descent.

Allison smiled weakly up at him, took some more deep, steadying breaths, tightened her hold on the rope and braced her feet against the side of the cave, and started moving slowly downward. With each step, her confidence grew. She was doing okay until she reached the open space with no wall to walk down. She lost her grip on one of the parts of the rope she was supposed to hold onto, and it moved out of her reach. She screamed in terror as she dropped toward the ground, but she fell little more than a foot before the brake on the harness kicked in. She spun around in circles as someone above lowered her the rest of the way down. When she was close to the ground, Ben caught hold of her. Trevor pushed him aside and unbuckled the harness. As soon as Allison stepped out of it, the harness disappeared back up the tunnel so the next student could come down. Trevor put his arms around her, and she leaned her head against his chest. Allison smelled smoke coming from Ben but ignored it. "I'm never doing that again as long as I live," she said.

Trevor held Allison close and kissed her forehead. "I hope you are never in a position where you have to," he murmured. Then he looked up and sniffed the air. "Do you smell that? It smells like smoke. I smelled it earlier too. Where in the world could that be coming from?"

It took some time to get everyone down the rope. The first students to come down sat on the sidelines with their backs against the rock wall, waiting for the others. Denzel was the last student to step out of the harness. Allison assumed he'd stayed at the top to help the others in the same way he'd helped her.

Phil Tanner stepped out of the harness and faced the students. "I'm glad to see you all made it down alive. The rest of today will be easier. Tomorrow we face the challenge of climbing back up that rope as we retrace our steps. All of last year's students managed to get back in one piece, and so will you."

"Cool," Denzel said, but most of the other students did not share his enthusiasm.

"Follow me," said Tanner. "We have a bit further to go before we stop for the night, but it will be much easier. This way to the lava tube."

The students fell in behind him. Ben watched Allison and waited to see what she would do. When he saw her take Trevor's hand, he turned and walked away.

The lava tube required the students to walk bent over, but other than that, it was easy going. At the end of the tube, there was a drop onto the floor of a large cavern that was breathtakingly beautiful. An earlier class had buried a couple of steel pegs into seams in the rock. A rope was attached to the pegs, and the class was rappelling down in the way they'd learned on the bluff near the school. It was a short easy rappel. Denzel led the way and Ben followed him down. When it was Allison's turn, Ben found himself holding his breath as he watched her come down, but she managed to do it without help. When she was down, and his breathing returned to normal, he noticed something different about the air. It was fresher and there was the faint smell of the sea.

They rested in the cavern, and Ben marveled at its beauty. Stalagmites grew up from the ground while stalactites hung from the ceiling. In some places, the two met and were fused together. When the light fell on them, they sparkled with multi-hued phosphorescence. It gave the whole cavern a magical appearance, and Ben was grateful to be able to see it with his own eyes. It was every bit as beautiful as anything he'd seen on the National Geographic programs his grandmother used to watch.

When it was time to continue, Tanner led them into another lava tube, which was longer than the previous one. Ben was growing very tired of walking hunched over when they came to a cavern where a small waterfall fell off to the left, after which it ran across the cavern and disappeared through a hole in the floor. A faint light was shining through the hole.

"Is this the same stream we saw earlier?" a student asked.

"I'm not sure. I've taken a boat out and seen where I believe it falls into the ocean, but it could be another stream. This cavern is where we'll stop for the night. The water probably won't hurt you, but I would use the straws that are in your backpack to drink from, just to be sure. Make yourself at home. I suggest the girls sleep on the left side of the cave and the boys on the right."

Phil Tanner untied his sleeping mat from his backpack. He moved to the middle of the cave and put it down after brushing aside some small rocks. The students knew without being told that he was the dividing line between male and female students. Ben lay his mat down about five feet away from the teacher. Denzel lay his down next to

Ben. They sat down on their mats and took out the food earmarked for their evening meal. Trevor came and placed his mat down between Ben and Tanner. Ben shifted around, so his back was toward Trevor.

4. Earthquake

Ben didn't know what woke him up. Perhaps a premonition? Maybe a slight shaking of the ground? But he was wide awake when the ground began to shake in earnest.

"Earthquake!" he yelled, bringing everyone except a student named Rudy instantly awake. Rudy always said he could sleep through anything. Clearly, he could sleep through a great deal, but not the rock that fell on his leg a few seconds after Ben raised the alarm. He woke up screaming in pain.

"Put your helmets on and get into the lava tube," Tanner yelled as he made his way over to Rudy.

Ben checked around for Allison and saw Trevor pulling her toward the tube. He then crawled over to Rudy to see if he could help. Tears streamed down Rudy's face. He was biting his lip to keep from crying out. There was blood on his right leg, and the lower half was not in line with the rest. Phil Tanner and Ben helped him sit up. The teacher supported him as Ben put Rudy's helmet on, then they carried him toward the lava tube between the two of them.

A few isolated rocks had come down with the first quake. As they walked toward the lava tube, a second quake hit that was more intense than the first one. The swaying ground caused Tanner to lose his balance. He fell, and Ben and Rudy fell with him. Rudy screamed out in pain. Trevor left the safety of the lava tube to come and help, followed by Denzel and Allison. Tanner told them to get back into the cave as the number of rocks falling from the cave ceiling increased. Ben did the only thing he knew to do. He transformed into a dragon and sheltered the humans under his body. Tanner stood and picked Rudy up and threw him over his shoulder. He carried Rudy while Ben protected them from rockfall as they moved toward the lava tube.

Something hit Ben hard between his wings, and he roared in pain. Every movement after that was painful, but he knew they couldn't stay where they were. Ben looked up and caught sight of the faces of his classmates. Mouths had dropped open, and eyes were wide. The only students not shocked were Denzel and Allison. It made Ben feel good to see the shock on Trevor's face. Allison had not told her boyfriend about his ability to transform into a dragon. Then he thought about how unhappy Miss Templeton would be that everyone now knew he was Dragonborn. That was his last thought before a large rock glanced off his head, and several more rained down on his body.

A moment before Ben fell to the ground, Tanner left the shelter of his body and ran to the lava tube with Rudy over his shoulder. A few smaller rocks pelted them as they ran. Behind them, rocks kept falling on Ben until he was completely covered. Allison couldn't see how anyone could survive that, not even a Dragonborn.

She started to go toward Ben, but Trevor held her back. "Ben would want you to wait a few minutes to make sure nothing else falls. When it stops, we'll go together."

Allison sank to her knees beside Rudy. It was hard to focus on him when all she could think of was Ben and whether he was still alive. However, she managed to heal Rudy and take away his pain. Not long after that, the ground stopped shaking.

"Trevor, please keep the rest of the students inside." Tanner stepped outside the safety of the lava tube and walked to where he'd last seen Ben. The students watched as he picked up a rock and threw it aside. He'd picked up a few more before Denzel came out and joined him in moving rocks. Several other students joined them even though the occasional rock was still falling.

When Ben's body, still in dragon form, was mostly free of rock, Allison dropped down on her knees beside him, her cheeks wet with tears. She wasn't the only student crying.

Allison put her hand on Ben, "He's still alive," she cried out. "But barely," she added.

Denzel clasped his hands in a sign that suggested prayers answered.

"I want everyone but Allison back inside the lava tube, and that includes you, Denzel," Tanner said.

Denzel backed up slowly, seemingly reluctant to do as asked.

"Trevor, take someone with you and go back the way we came to see what the situation is," Tanner ordered.

"Denzel, why don't you come with me," Trevor suggested quietly.

Denzel looked at Trevor and then looked back to where Ben's body lay on the ground. It looked like he was going to object, but then he nodded in agreement.

The two of them pushed their way past the other students sheltering in the lava tube.

Allison closed her eyes and focused her powers on Ben. She discovered a broken back and wings and severely damaged kidneys. Though unsure she could heal a dragon this severely wounded, Allison knew she had to try because this wasn't just a dragon; this was her friend. Ben was her best friend if she didn't count Trevor.

Allison started by healing his kidneys before turning her attention to his back. These were the things that needed to be done for Ben to survive and be able to walk again. He could live with two broken wings or arms if he were able to transform, but he'd never get out of this cave system in either dragon or human form with a broken back and damaged kidneys. As Allison sent her healing power into him, she could feel her energy draining away. Her strength was limited, especially after healing Rudy, but she had to try. Her hands were shaking, and her legs felt weak. It would be so much easier to treat him if Ben was in his human form, but if he transformed now, he would not survive his injuries. Allison decided to heal him to the point where it was safe for him to transform.

Ben's back was nearly mended, and his kidney function almost restored when Allison woke him up. As he came awake, Ben howled in pain. Allison feared the noise would knock more rocks down on them.

"Ben," Alison said. "I'm healing you. I know this is hard when you are in so much pain, but can you transform back into a human? It will be easier to complete your healing."

Ben lifted his head and groaned. "It hurts too much."

"I need you to do this, so it isn't so hard to heal you," Allison said. "You know I'll keep trying no matter what." Her voice quivered.

Ben transformed into his human form, cried out in pain, and then was silent. Allison touched him and realized he had passed out. She finished healing his back so he could be safely moved. Mr. Tanner called over one of the students, and they carried Ben into the safety of the lava tube. A couple of girls from the class came out and helped Allison stand when they noticed she was having a hard time getting to her feet.

Once she was inside the tube, Allison fell to her knees beside Ben. She was dizzy and having a hard time focusing, but she sent her power into him to finish his healing. Allison discovered that not only were his arms broken, but he had a broken leg and a couple of broken ribs. She healed his arms, his leg, and one of his broken ribs before falling into unconsciousness herself.

It took almost an hour for Trevor and Denzel to come back from checking out their return path.

Trevor dropped to his knees when he saw Allison lying on the ground beside Ben. He cradled her head in his lap. "What happened?" he asked.

"She was healing Ben, and I think she gave too much of herself," Tanner said.

Trevor placed his fingers on Allison's neck so he could check her pulse. It was weak and erratic. Trevor felt himself grow very angry with the teacher. It was his job to protect the students, even if it meant protecting them from themselves. He tried to control his anger but couldn't. "You shouldn't have let her do that," he finally said to the teacher. His voice was loud inside the enclosed space of the lava tube.

"I would have had to physically hold her back to stop her, and I wasn't prepared to do that," Tanner said.

Trevor was about to say more, but Denzel jumped in. "We've got a problem. Rocks are blocking the way out. We moved some, but no matter how many we moved, there were always more."

"We can't go back the way we came," Trevor said. "Is there another way out?"

"I was afraid of that," Tanner said. "Those rock formations are beautiful but fragile. I don't know if there is another way out, but we need to do our best to find one."

"We need to do it soon," Trevor said. "Allison needs help."

"Would you like me to check and see if there's a way out by going forward?" Denzel asked.

"Allison! What's wrong with Allison?" Ben asked as he pushed himself up on his elbows.

"She drained herself of energy healing you," Trevor said with a note of accusation in his voice. He resented Ben despite knowing he wasn't to blame.

"There wasn't another way out when we explored these caves when I was a student," Phil Tanner gestured to the cave they had been sleeping in when the earthquake started, "but who knows what the situation is now. Trevor, you stay here with Allison. Denzel and I will check and see what's

up ahead. The lava tube did continue on the other side of
the cavern, but it dead-ended. Maybe that's changed."

Ben pushed himself up from the ground. "I need to go
with you. There are places a dragon can go that a human
can't."

"I'm not sure that's wise," Tanner said. "You're not fully
recovered, and if you have a setback, Allison will not be
able to help you."

"I know, but we have to find a way out, and a fair
amount of rock can fall on me in my dragon form without
serious injury. You, on the other hand…," Ben left the last
sentence unfinished. No one needed him to tell them that
human bodies were vulnerable to injury from falling rock.

"Okay, Ben. Let's go see what we can find." Tanner
pushed himself up from the ground. "It's been years since I
went past this point in the cave system. Perhaps with any
luck, the lava tube will lead us outside."

There was still the occasional rock falling as Tanner
walked across the cavern. He shone the light from his
helmet on the ground as he made his way to where he
thought the tunnel continued on. When he didn't find it,
Tanner realized it must be behind a pile of rock that had
come down with the earthquake. He started to pull rocks
aside, but it was too slow for one person alone. Tanner had
no choice but to call Ben and Denzel. He had told them to
wait in the lava tube until he'd found the entrance. He

hadn't wanted them exposed to falling rock any longer than they needed to be.

"Okay, Ben and Denzel, I found the tunnel, but we need to move rocks to get into it." Tanner watched as two lights started walking across the cavern toward him. Once the two boys arrived, they quickly moved enough rock to be able to crawl into the tunnel.

Tanner let out a sigh of relief once they were inside, and he didn't need to worry about rocks coming down from high above them. They hadn't gone very far when Tanner stopped walking. "Do you feel that?" he asked.

At first, his question was met with silence.

"I felt it," Ben said. "And it smells like the ocean. There must be fresh air coming from somewhere. Maybe we will find a way out this way."

They walked a little further on. Phil Tanner realized it was getting lighter. He turned off the light on his helmet to check, and he definitely could still faintly see the way in front of him. He hurried along the lava tube. When the tunnel turned, there was a bright light in front of him. He found it impossible to see after being in the dark so long. He squinted his eyes as he kept walking. He stepped forward only to discover there was no rock beneath his feet. He would have fallen if Denzel hadn't grabbed the back of his shirt. As his vision improved, he saw the chasm in front of him that he'd almost fallen into.

"Thank you, Denzel," Tanner said once his feet were on solid rock again. He looked out across to the other side of the chasm, where the tube continued. The gulf between the two sides was too far to jump. When he looked up, there was light coming from a crack in the rock above them. The early morning sun was shining through it. "Can you fly up there?" he asked Ben.

Ben stepped forward and looked up. "No, I can't. The sides become too narrow for my wings. Maybe I can fly across to the other side and see if there is a way out further on." Ben pointed across to where the tube continued.

"Let's hope there is." Tanner could hear the stress he felt in his voice. He was more worried than he ever remembered being. He felt responsible for the students trapped inside the mountain with him.

5. The Lava Tube

Ben was too big to enter the lava tube on the other side of the chasm in his dragon form. He would need to dive toward it as a dragon but transform into a human before he reached it. Transform too soon, and Ben would fall toward the rocks below. Too late and he risked breaking a wing on the rock surrounding the tube. It was going to be tricky, and the stakes were high. However, Ben was his friends 'only hope for getting out of this place unless someone came to rescue them. It wasn't impossible. The Guardian could send Chosen from another world to help them, or Miss Templeton could send a rescue party.

He threw himself into the chasm and transformed into a dragon. The space between the two sides was not very wide. He let himself fall and then flew upward toward the cave. He was almost there when an image of himself laying broken at the bottom of the chasm flashed through his mind. He knew it was what would happen if he didn't do this exactly right. He beat his wings in desperation to change the direction of his flight. Instead of flying into the cave mouth, he flew upward as far as he could go before it became too narrow. He looped around and approached the cave from above. It was a better angle. Just before he crashed into the rock, he transformed into a human. The momentum he'd created with his dragon wings caused him to hit the cave floor with more force than his human body liked. He stumbled forward and fell hard onto his knees. He cried in pain, not just from his knees, but because he'd jarred his broken rib. He pushed himself up, grateful to be alive.

A few hundred feet ahead, he was heartened by the feel of a stiff breeze on his cheek. Ahead of him was a circle of light that became brighter with every step he took. Soon he stood at a cave entrance looking out over the ocean. At the beginning of this island's life, lava had poured down into the sea from this tube. Tanner had told him that the end of the tube had been plugged with lava when he explored this far years ago. Now it ended with a cave overlooking the ocean. He looked down and noticed waves crashing at least sixty feet below him on newly fallen rock. The earthquake must have caused this part of the island to break away. Ben turned and ran back to where he'd left the other two to tell them the good news.

"I need you to do two things," Tanner told Ben. "I want you to go and get one of the sailboards and whatever rope you can find. Also, look for a log or, better yet, a plank that can bridge the crevice. And do your best not to be seen. Miss Templeton is going to have a fit when she discovers if she doesn't already know that the whole class has learned you're Dragonborn."

Thinking about it, Ben was sure Miss Templeton already knew.

"I'm surprised the Guardian hasn't sent Chosen from one of the other worlds to rescue us," Denzel said.

"I'm sure the Guardian would have if we couldn't rescue ourselves. And thanks to the fact that we have our very own dragon, I believe it is possible."

As Tanner said those words, Ben felt certainty replace the doubt that had wedged in his heart. He could do this. He could rescue his class.

Ben was soon flying around the mountainous island looking for the beach where they'd left their sailboards. He saw no sign of it in his first pass and concluded that big waves caused by the earthquake had washed everything out to sea. Ben wondered what happened to Mr. Smith. He didn't like the crusty teacher but still wanted to find him alive.

Ben flew until he spotted bright red and yellow boards floating in the ocean. He picked up one and carried it to a flat spot halfway up the island mountain. The sail was missing, and there was no rope. However, all he had to do was find the cave where they'd entered the mountain and take the rope they used to climb up to it. He left the board and looked for something that would span the crevice, wide enough for his classmates to walk safely on. Much of what had been on the beaches was now floating in the ocean.

Ben found the perfect piece of lumber. One that in a previous life had been part of a pier. He carried it directly to the mouth of the lava tube and pitched it in without transforming. He still needed rope, so he flew away to look for it. It was time to find the cave they'd entered yesterday.

Nothing looked the same as it had the day before. Many of the beaches were no longer there. He flew slowly along the shoreline, looking for the cave mouth and the rope that should still be hanging in front of it. He finally found it and was about to burn through the rope when a voice boomed out. "Taylor, if you're looking for me, I'm here."

Ben looked up and saw Mr. Smith in the mouth of the cave.

"I'm glad you're alive, sir. Can you climb down, and I'll come and get you after the others are safe? I need that rope to carry Allison back to Miss Templeton."

"What's wrong with Allison?"

"She used too much energy healing me."

"What happened? Never mind, I can hear your story later."

"Good idea. The other students are trapped and need my help."

"Here's the thing, I managed to climb with one hand and a hook, but it wasn't easy, and my hand was hurt." Mr.

Smith held out his flesh and blood hand, and Ben could see the skin on his palm had been stripped away.

"I'll fly in close to the rock below you. Drop onto my back, and I'll take you somewhere safe."

"I've always wanted to take a flight by dragonwing."

Ben flew under him, and Mr. Smith grabbed the rope with his hook and swung out so he could drop down onto his back. Ben then used his dragonfire to separate the rope from the tree. He carried Mr. Smith to the spot where he'd left the sailboard. He dropped the teacher off and picked up the sailboard before flying to the mouth of the lava tube. Ben tossed the board and rope in, then circled and flew directly at the cave mouth. Once again, he needed to transform at just the right moment so that the forward movement would carry his human body into the mouth of the cave.

The wood plank was heavy, but he tied the rope around it and dragged it toward the crevice. When he arrived, he threw the free end of the rope across to the other side. Denzel caught it, and he and Tanner used it to pull the plank toward them while Ben pushed it. He put downward pressure on the plank as he pushed to prevent it from falling into the crevice. Soon the plank was in place, and they had a makeshift bridge.

"Stay there," Ben said. "While I go and get the sailboard for Allison."

"We'll send the students over one at a time then," Tanner said. "Starting with Allison."

"I'll need help to get her safely away," Ben said. "But once you've helped me with that, only one person at a time should be on this side of the chasm. It's in the process of breaking away from the mountain and could fall at any time. It will come down if there is another quake.

They tied Allison to the sailboard with the rope. Trevor and Tanner carried her across the plank to the place where the lava tube ended. Tanner felt he needed to see what the situation was, and Trevor insisted he carry Allison.

"What's the best way to do this?" Tanner asked when they were looking out over the ocean.

"I'll jump out and transform, and you can throw me the ropes," Ben said. "I need to have both ropes in my hand when I pull her out so the board can be kept level."

They had secured the rope around both the front and back end of the board.

Ben jumped as far out as he could, transformed, and arced back around. He missed the ropes on his first try, but the second time he caught them in what would have been his hands if he was in human form. Ben pulled the sailboard straight out of the lava tube toward the open ocean before turning in a gentle arc toward Fairhaven. He wanted to get Allison to Miss Templeton quickly. She would know what to do.

As he neared the school, he noticed the wooden pier floating out on the ocean along with some of the boats. Other boats were resting on the bottom of the ocean near shore. A few others had been deposited on land in places the waves did not usually reach. More than one was damaged beyond repair.

Miss Templeton was waiting for him when he landed. "What has taken you so long? Allison needed to be here an hour ago."

Ben started to answer.

"Never mind," Miss Templeton continued. "Go back and get the others. I'll look after Allison."

Ben would have liked nothing better than to stay and make sure Allison would be okay, but he had no choice but to go.

As he took to the air, he looked down and saw several startled faces looking up at him. The secret was most definitely out. He doubted Miss Templeton would even try to erase the memories of so many people who now knew he was Dragonborn.

He was glad they knew. He could now tell them about his time on Lushaka and Zargon and the true story of what happened on Farne. Instead of thinking of him as a dork, the students in his school would know how special he was. That last thought caught him up short— where did it come from? *Was that the kind of thinking that got his great uncle*

Zork in trouble? Did Zork start to think he was extra special and more important than anyone else? It was cool to transform into a dragon, but there were temptations that dragons faced because of their unique abilities. When he thought about it, his mother had spoken of this very thing. She said the Dragonborn could quickly become arrogant and a danger to the people around them because of their special powers and greater strength.

When Ben returned to the crevice in human form, he found the entire class waiting to take their turn at crossing the plank and flying away.

"Allison is being looked after by the Watcher," Ben said. Glancing at Trevor, he noticed the relief on his face.

"Good," Tanner said.

Trevor turned away from Ben and said nothing.

"Is there somewhere close by where you can drop students off so we can get everyone out quickly?" Tanner asked. "It should be a stable piece of land high enough up from the ocean in case another big wave comes in."

"I've already chosen the perfect place," Ben said. "I've taken Mr. Smith there."

"Good," Tanner said. "We'll keep people on this side of the crevice until it's their turn to fly. Who would like to go first?"

Denzel stepped forward before the teacher finished speaking. Mr. Tanner smiled at Denzel, who was his best student in the grade eleven Physical Education class.

"Denzel, I'd like you to wait here with Trevor until everyone else is across. I'll go along with whoever else volunteers to go first and stay at the cave opening to help people safely leave the mouth of the cave. So, who other than Denzel would like to go first?"

Roku, a rather shy Japanese girl known to have a crush on Ben, stepped forward and walked onto the wooden plank. With one careful step after another, she crossed over the crevice and waited on the other side for Ben and the Physical Education teacher.

Ben was surprised. He hadn't expected Roku to be the first to volunteer.

"Count slowly to... what do you think, Ben?" Tanner asked.

"Four hundred."

"Count slowly to four hundred and then send the next student over."

"There are three ways of doing this," Ben said to Roku as they walked. "I can hold onto you, and the two of us can jump away from the cave mouth together. But if you chicken out at the last moment, we could end up in trouble. You can hold onto my back, but that might be tricky to do as I transform, or I can jump out, transform, and swing back around as a dragon to catch you when you jump."

"What would you prefer?" Roku asked.

"The third option," Ben said.

"I choose the third option then," Roku looked at Ben and smiled shyly.

"Let's do this for all the students if they're not too afraid," Tanner said from where he walked behind them. "When you fly by, I'll cue each student to jump at the right time."

Ben flung himself off the end of the cave and quickly transformed.

"This isn't going to be easy," Phil Tanner said to Roku as he looked down at the waves crashing on the rocks below. "But you can trust Ben. He won't let you fall." Tanner hoped what he was saying was true. He doubted Ben had ever done this before, and it might be more challenging than he realized.

As Ben approached the mouth of the cave, Tanner told Roku to be ready, but when he was close enough, she couldn't make herself jump. She teetered on the edge for a moment before stepping back. Phil Tanner didn't blame her. It was a terrifying thing to do.

"We'll try again," Tanner said.

"I'm sorry. I'll jump next time," Roku promised.

Ben flew around again, and this time when Tanner said jump, the girl jumped. Tanner held his breath as Roku sailed through the air and began to fall toward the ocean. If she hit the rocks, she would be dead. He admired her for not screaming in terror. He wasn't sure he could keep himself from doing so. He only let out his breath when Ben caught Roku and lifted her into the air. Phil watched as she was carried up and over the island and out of sight. He was not looking forward to seeing the rest of his students make this dangerous jump. He hoped he dared to make it himself when his turn came.

Tanner hoped it was his imagination, but he felt the sliver of rock he was standing on shudder. Had there just been another earthquake, or was this bit of the mountain still caught up in processes that had begun with the last quake? There was no doubt it was breaking away from the main mountain, but he hoped it would wait just a little while longer before crumbling into the ocean.

Most of the students managed to throw themselves out of the cave. Rudy couldn't do it by any of the three methods Ben had suggested. He ended up sitting on the ledge while Ben flew upward along the face of the rock. Ben grabbed Rudy with his back feet as he flew by. When they arrived at the place where he'd left the other students, Ben had to drop Rudy to the ground before he could land.

Only Trevor and Phil Tanner were still waiting to be rescued when there was a small aftershock. The ground under their feet tilted toward the ocean.

"We need to go across the crevice and wait on the stable side of the mountain," Tanner said. He took off running through the lava tube with Trevor right behind him. It seemed to Tanner that the angle increased as they ran.

They arrived in time to see the plank they'd placed over the crevice fall into the widening gulf. There was no way to get to the other side. The sliver of the mountain they were standing on was falling into the ocean and taking them with it. They were both going to die. "I'm sorry, Trevor," Tanner said.

"It's not your fault," Trevor replied. "Never thought the day would come when I would long to see Ben Taylor return."

Trevor and Tanner stood on either side of the lava tube with their backs resting against the rock wall. The mountain shuddered. Rocks were falling around them. A few smaller rocks pelted them, but they weren't hit by anything large enough to knock them off the ledge they stood on. They were tilting toward the ocean, and the tilt was growing. Any minute and this part of the mountain would fall into the sea. Tanner closed his eyes. He didn't want to know what was coming. He didn't see the dragon claws that reached out and plucked them off the rock. As they rose into the air, Phil Tanner noticed that the space above them, which Ben had not been able to fly through earlier, was now wide enough for a dragon.

Ben took them to the first possible landing spot and suggested they climb onto his back for the trip to join the others. Within five minutes they arrived. Ben carried the students and teachers on his back two at a time from there to the school.

6. Bad News

At supper that night, there was more noise in the dining hall than usual. Ben knew he was the topic of some of the conversations. If people weren't talking about him, they were talking about where they were when the earthquake hit.

There were more people than usual crowded around the table where Denzel and Ben usually sat. Ben found it hard to eat with all the questions that were coming at him fast and furious. He was worried about Allison, who was not at her usual table, and he didn't feel like answering questions.

The students who didn't know the school's true purpose were more than a little overcome by the reality of a dragon in their midst. Those who did know were aware that there was a world with transforming dragons on it. What they didn't know was what one was doing at their school. The excitement of those who did not know the school's real purpose would only last until Miss Templeton erased their memory. *Would she try to erase everyone's mind?* Ben wondered if she could. He hoped not. He liked people knowing he was Dragonborn even if he didn't feel like answering their questions at the moment.

He had just made up his mind to go upstairs and see if he could find out what happened to Allison when she walked through the door. Her face was pale, and she was slower than usual, but she was moving under her own steam. Ben was about to go to Allison when Trevor arrived and embraced her in a hug. Ben watched as Allison closed her eyes and rested her head on Trevor's shoulder. He turned away as he couldn't stand seeing the two of them together. After supper, he felt a need to be alone, so he went to the stable and saddled Rusty.

When Ben got back from his ride, Denzel was in the room they shared.

"A couple of the teachers were in the common room after supper," Denzel said. "They had the TV on. Somebody got a picture of you and sent it to the news."

Ben closed his eyes and bowed his head for a moment. Then he looked up at Denzel. "Miss Templeton's not going to be happy about that. Her biggest fear is someone coming around, asking about strange happenings. She's afraid they'll start asking about a dragon and continue to ask questions about what a school is doing in such an isolated spot and why they've never heard of it before."

"She likely won't even let you fly on dark moonless nights until she's sure all of this has blown over."

"No doubt," Ben said, feeling his heart sink. He loved the midnight flights which strengthened his wings and kept his dragon body physically fit.

"I've got other news you're not going to like," Denzel said.

"What's that?" Ben asked.

"While Allison was with the Watcher, she was tested. She's going to Mellish with you and Trevor."

Ben couldn't help himself; fire and smoke erupted from within. The flame barely missed Denzel. It curled the outdated wallpaper just behind him.

"Wow, Ben, you have to chill out. You can't be this way if the three of you are trying to fix whatever problem Mellish has together."

"You're right. I'll see Miss Templeton tomorrow and tell her I have a problem going with Trevor and Allison. I'm not looking forward to the lecture she'll give me about not getting romantically involved with other students."

"You're not romantically involved," Denzel pointed out.

"Yes, I know, and that's the real problem. Allison and I are meant to be together." Ben's voice cracked.

"She doesn't see it that way, and it would be better if you didn't either," Denzel said.

Ben could see the sympathy on his friend's face. He turned away, so Denzel didn't see the moisture in the corner of his eyes.

Ben wasn't able to see Miss Templeton the following day. She was busy erasing the memories of some of the students in tenth grade and all the students in the ninth grade. The good news was that she had decided to let those who knew the school's real purpose keep their memory of him being a dragon.

By the following day, he almost changed his mind about talking to her. The kids in his school were making his life miserable. Some of them weren't bad; they were just full of questions about what it was like to be a dragon. Others wanted a ride sometime when the night was dark. Others had heard he could breathe fire even in his human form and were trying to provoke him enough to see some smoke.

When Ben finally got to see Miss Templeton, it didn't go well. "I would prefer not to go to Mellish if Trevor is going," he said.

"And why's that?" she asked.

"I don't think we'll work together well," Ben said.

"And what reasons do you have for believing that?"

"I don't trust him to have my back."

"Why would you say that?"

"I don't think he likes it that Allison and I are friends."

"And why would you say that?"

"He thinks Allison is his girlfriend."

"From what I understand, she is."

"I thought it was against the rules to have a girlfriend?"

"We discourage romantic relationships but find them impossible to stop altogether."

"Well, I don't want to go to Mellish if both Trevor and Allison are going."

"I trust them to do what is right. Besides, the Guardian has chosen the three of you, and the three of you should go."

Ben left Miss Templeton's office frustrated. Although when he thought about it, he didn't want Allison to go off-world without him. Someone needed to be there to protect her, and he didn't trust Trevor to do it.

7. Departure Day

On the day of their departure, Trevor and Allison were already in Miss Templeton's office when Ben arrived.

Allison was sitting in the stuffed leather chair, and Trevor was sitting on the arm of the same chair. Ben was annoyed that Miss Templeton allowed Trevor to sit there. Why hadn't she told him to either sit on the metal chair or get one of the wooden ones stacked against the wall? He gingerly sat on the unique metal chair with its Celtic knots, knowing it meant he would be the first to receive whatever gifts the Guardian of the Six Worlds would hand out for this mission.

Miss Templeton pushed a cup of tea across her desk toward him. Allison and Trevor already had cups in front of them. The principal leaned back in her chair, closed her eyes, and sat in silence for a minute before speaking. "I have just learned that there will be someone from Lushaka going to Mellish with you." Miss Templeton turned toward Ben. "Ben, you know her. Charla is going with you."

Ben was shocked when he heard Charla was joining them. The last time he'd seen her, she had been far from ready. He guessed their mission was not very dangerous if the Guardian was sending the mermaid. He was surprised then by the Watcher's next words.

"This is a very challenging mission. You may never face another as dangerous as this one."

"Why is the Guardian sending students still in training then?" Allison asked.

"I'm not sure. Perhaps because the Guardian has a lot of faith in the three of you, all of you have off-world experience and have proven your courage and ability." Miss Templeton paused to take a drink of tea. "I must tell you this. Others have come; some have died, others are in prison, and a few have joined the enemy in a rebellion against the Guardian. Perhaps one reason you're going is the Guardian knows your hearts are true."

"There's a rebellion against the Guardian?" Allison asked in surprise. "Their Watcher must be so ashamed."

"The Watcher of Mellish is leading the rebellion," Miss Templeton said. "Grek has gone rogue and is using the power the Guardian has given him to rule the world he was supposed to protect. Grek is talking as if he were a God worthy of people's worship. He wants their total and unquestioning obedience. Grek has moved honest people with integrity out of public office and put shysters in their place. He is making himself and his friends wealthy at the expense of the poor. He has moved out of the school for training Chosen into the palace the President usually lives in. The Guardian's Medallion means he will live and rule for centuries unless we stop him."

"Grek has control over the whole world?" Ben asked in shock. In his research on the Six Worlds, he had never heard of a Watcher going rogue, and he had never thought what it would mean if one did. Although on the last world he'd been to, the Watcher was very eccentric; one might even say somewhat mad.

"Mellish has a small population because it has little arable land. So, it's not as hard as it would be on other worlds to gain control. Here on Earth, it would be nearly impossible." Miss Templeton paused and took another sip of tea. "There are Resistance groups on Mellish. Your first step will be to get in touch with one of them. They will have a better idea of how to stop Grek than I do."

"How are we to get to the Resistance? Doesn't Grek control the room of portals?" Trevor asked.

"He has soldiers watching it. He can no longer use the portals to send people to other worlds, but we can still send the Chosen to Mellish through them."

"Wait! Won't Grek have soldiers guarding the pool of arrival?" Ben asked.

"Yes, you will be arrested when you arrive. There's nothing we can do about that."

"But what good will we be in prison?" Ben asked.

Miss Templeton sipped her tea before answering. "The Guardian knows the situation you are going into but still has selected you to go, which means you have a good chance of succeeding even if your first destination is jail."

"When a Watcher goes rogue, don't they lose power?" Allison asked.

"Yes and no," Miss Templeton said. "Thankfully, the chair no longer bestows gifts. Only the Medallion continues to have a limited amount of power that it bestows regardless of the worthiness of the one who has it. Thankfully, some of the Medallion's power has faded because Grek has lost his connection to the Guardian. For example, he needs to be connected to the Guardian to have a mystical connection to his world that would allow him to know where the Resistance is. The Medallion's power is now limited, but it is still able to keep him alive long past his normal expiration date. And while his powers are blunted, he is still very dangerous."

"We need to find a way to take it away from him then," Trevor said.

"Yes, I expect that's at least part of your mission," Miss Templeton replied. "Your first step is to find the Resistance so they can help you. Although I don't think they'll be hard to find. You'll likely meet them shortly after you go through the portal. Truehaven is now a prison, and both Resistance and Chosen are kept there."

"That's terrible," Allison said. "It's the complete opposite of what the Guardian intended when creating Truehaven as a school for the Chosen."

"You are so right, Allison," Miss Templeton said. "I wish I could give you a reason to hope that you will escape arrest. I can't. Several have gone, and thus far everyone has been prevented from doing what they were sent to do." Miss Templeton was silent for a minute before continuing. "My job is not to second guess the Guardian; my job is to send the ones the Guardian chooses if they are willing to be sent."

"Why can't we use a gateway instead?" Ben asked. "I don't want to end up in prison again."

"There are no gateways on Mellish that you can connect with, so there is no way to avoid being arrested. I don't want to send you, but it is essential to get the Medallion away from Grek. We need to get it away from him so we can give it to a new Watcher. The Guardian has determined that you three have the best chance of success of the Chosen who are available at this time."

"We still have the choice as to whether we go, right?" Trevor asked.

"What's the matter, Trev? Are you scared?" Ben sneered, using the name Allison and Trevor's friends used. As soon as the words were out of his mouth, he felt ashamed of them.

"No more than you are," Trevor said. "I was not asking for myself, but for you."

"I'm sure I don't need to tell you two how important it is that the team work together. You must put aside your differences. Do you think you can do so?" asked Miss Templeton.

"Yes," Trevor said quickly.

Ben didn't answer right away, and when he did, it was with a barely perceptible nod of his head.

"Now shall we find out what gifts the Guardian has for you?" Miss Templeton stood and walked over to where Ben sat. She laid her hands on the top of his head, and light burst forth from the Guardian's special chair. The brightness of it caused Ben to close his eyes. He opened them again when Miss Templeton said he was going to be a wizard. Her words thrilled him. It was a gift of power and one that everyone wanted. Ben was pleased that he, rather than Trevor, would be the group's wizard. Previously, Trevor had received this gift every time he went off-world. Ben was surprised at the gift he received next. It was the gift of being able to shrink in size. He wondered how he would put that gift to use.

Ben glanced at Trevor as he pushed himself out of the special chair. It was hard for him to keep from smirking when he noticed the disappointment on Trevor's face. He wouldn't be the wizard this time out. Ben would be.

"Well," Miss Templeton said. "In all my years as a Watcher, I've never seen the gift of being able to change your size before. I can think of many times when it would have been useful, but it was never given until now. I wonder what gifts are waiting for the other two."

"Why don't you go next?" Trevor asked Allison.

Allison sat down on the elaborate metal chair, and Miss Templeton touched the top of her head. The light was so bright that Ben closed his eyes for a moment before reopening them slowly.

"That's unusual," Miss Templeton said. "Allison has been given only one gift. Her healing gift is greatly expanded. She will be able to heal a lot of people before she runs out of power. She can also pass on the healing gift to another person. Chose that person wisely and well, Allison."

A smile lit up Allison's face.

When she got up, Trevor sat down. Ben had only received two gifts because of his permanent gift of being able to transform into a dragon. Trevor would receive three gifts, and Ben hoped they would be dorky ones like being the ability to see in the dark. He knew that wouldn't be the case when the light that came forth from the chair was even brighter than it had been for him and Allison. Ben held his breath as Miss Templeton announced the gifts he'd received.

Trevor also had the wizarding gift. Ben scowled but quickly forced a smile onto his face as he waited to see what the other gifts would be. When the second gift was given, there was an explosion of light.

"Well, I've never seen anything like this," Miss Templeton said. "The Guardian is digging deep to stop Grek."

"What's my second gift?" Trevor asked.

"One that is rarely given along with wizarding. I've only seen these two gifts given to one person at the same time once before today," Miss Templeton moved back to her chair and sat down. "Your second gift gave birth to the superman legend. You will be very strong and fast. You can't fly, but it will feel like you can because of your ability to jump great distances. Not only that, but your body will be able to endure a great deal of abuse."

"Will I have X-ray eyes?" Trevor asked.

"That's only in comic books," Miss Templeton said.

They waited for a third gift, but none came.

"I think," Miss Templeton hesitated. "That these two gifts together count as three."

Ben wanted the others to think he was happy about the distribution of gifts, so he kept a smile on his face. When Miss Templeton turned and stared at him, he knew she wasn't fooled. "Ben, I want to have a private word with you while the others go to the Room of Portals," she said.

8. Capture

Charla arrived through the in-coming portal on Mellish an instant before the three Chosen from Earth. Her coming went unnoticed because she'd used the gift of shrinking and was about the size of a housefly. The signal which announced her arrival was hidden by the alarm for the others. The appearance of three full-sized Chosen caused a large wave that sent her tumbling through the water to hit the side of the pool.

Waves washed over her as she watched guards reach out with sticks that had loops on the end of them. The guard closest to her dropped the loop over Ben's head and used the attached stick to drag him toward the edge of the pool. Other guards did the same to Trevor and Allison. They dragged Ben right to where Charla waited. She reached out and grabbed a few strands of Ben's wet hair.

If the guards looked closely, they would see her, but she trusted they would be too busy with the big off-worlders to notice the tiny one. She had wondered if she would be the only one with the gift of being able to shrink. If the Chosen from Earth had it, why did they all come through the portal full size?

As they pulled Ben roughly out of the water, the strands of hair Charla hung onto swung back and forth past his ear. When his head tilted in the right direction, Charla let go of his hair and jumped into Ben's ear, where she was less likely to be seen. She slid down face first into a pool of water in his ear canal.

Ben didn't appreciate the water and a bug sized Charla in his ear. He tilted his head and shook it. Charla would have been washed out along with the water if she hadn't reached out to grab hold of a bump in front of her, which she used to pull herself further down into the ear canal. She had to let Ben know she was in his ear, so he didn't keep trying to dislodge her.

"Gross, Ben! Don't you ever clean your ears?" She shouted when she realized she was holding onto a hardened pile of ear wax.

"What?" Ben said, almost immediately. The vibrations from his voice shook Charla, and she held on tight despite being grossed out by what she was holding onto.

"No speaking," one of the guards said to Ben.

Everything went dark, and when Charla looked over her shoulder, she could not see out of the ear canal.

"Nod if they put something over your head," she shouted.

Ben nodded his head forward and back, and Charla slid first this way and then that.

"A smaller nod next time."

Ben gave a very slight nod.

"Why aren't you transforming into a dragon?" Charla asked.

"Can't," Ben whispered.

"Have you tried?"

Ben nodded.

"Something's blocking the use of your gifts?"

Ben nodded again.

"It must be the metal loop they dropped over you because I'm still able to use mine."

Ben nodded again.

"If I jump to the ground from this high up, I'll break something. I'm going to see if I can climb down your body and get to a position where it is safer. If I need you to take a fall to get me closer to the ground, I'll prick you. Do you understand?"

Ben hesitated and then gave a very slight nod.

Charla crawled out of Ben's ear. She jumped into the gunny-sack-like material that covered his head. It was belted around his neck and made the perfect slide. She crawled along until she found a spot where it wasn't as tight as other places and wiggled her way through. There were a few strands of wet hair hanging out from under the sack. Charla climbed down on one until she could safely drop onto Ben's shirt collar.

She stopped and took in her surroundings. A guard was dragging Ben along by the pole attached to the loop around his neck. He tied Ben's wrists together in front of him. Trevor and Allison also had their wrists bound, and guards were pulling them along behind them. Each of them had a sack over their heads, so they couldn't see where they were going. Not that there was anything to see. They were being walked down a long corridor where they passed the occasional closed door. They came to an elevator and took it down a level.

Charla started moving along Ben's collar until she got to the buttons, then she worked her way down the buttonhole side of the shirt. It was slow progress, and half of her body was visible to anyone who looked closely. As she reached the second button, she noticed a thread coming loose. That hanging thread gave Charla an idea. She decided to use it as a rope to rappel down. With any luck, it would slowly unravel when she put her weight on it. If it didn't, she would increase in size until it did. She planned to pull the thread through the buttonhole to use it on the inside of his shirt where she wouldn't be visible. If the thread was too short to get her all the way down to his waistline, she felt confident that her fall would halt at the place where his shirt tucked into his jeans.

Holding tight to the shirt with her left hand, she reached out for the edge of the buttonhole with her right hand. Once she had a good hold, she let go of the fabric in her left hand and swung herself over. She pulled herself up so she could stand on the thick, zigzagged thread. Once she was standing, she grabbed the outside edge of the button to steady herself as she reached around it for the thread with her other hand. For the first time, she found herself appreciating the stickiness of the ear wax still on her hands. It helped her hold onto the smooth round button. She caught hold of the thread and jerked it toward herself to see if it would unravel, but nothing happened. She couldn't put enough pressure on it by pulling with only one hand. She wasn't stable enough to put any more weight on it. It was hard enough to keep her balance on the buttonhole as Ben walked. She had reluctantly decided that using the thread was not going to work, and she needed to come up with a new plan when Ben stumbled, and her feet slipped off the buttonhole. If she hadn't grabbed the thread with both hands, she would have fallen to the ground. The thread unraveled and left her hanging just underneath the button. She was not on the inside of the shirt as she'd planned, but on the outside. She needed to get out of sight as soon as possible. The thread had stopped unraveling, and she couldn't reach the buttonhole above her or the side of the shirt. The only thing she had to hold onto was the thread.

When she tried to climb back up, it started to unravel again and then stopped. She was stuck halfway between two buttons. Since climbing up hadn't worked, she decided to risk becoming bigger, so there was more weight on the thread. She just hoped no one looked her way. She grew in size until she felt the thread start to unravel again. When she started going too fast, she shrunk her body down in size, so there was less weight. The second time she tried that, the momentum slowed, but she was still spinning downwards. Charla worried there would not be enough thread to take her to the ground. It wouldn't be a problem inside the shirt, but it was on the outside. If she dropped from where she was, it would be the equivalent of falling ten stories. She wouldn't survive such a fall unless she grew large enough that everyone would be able to see her. Could she call on a gift that came with being a wizard? She wasn't sure and didn't want to try for the first time when the stakes were so high.

The thread was completely loose from the button before she reached the waistband of Ben's jeans. Her fall was now out of control. She reached for the waistband, missed, but managed to catch hold of the pocket. She was dangling from it when she looked up to see the button hurtling toward her. She barely avoided being hit as it whizzed by. She pulled herself up and over the top of the pocket so she could climb inside it. Half of her body was inside and half outside when they arrived at a door guarded by two soldiers. The door looked out of place. Everything else was old and made of stone or finely crafted wood, but the door was new and made of metal. It had a small window with bars in it and was in the middle of a freshly constructed wall. Grek had turned the ancient school for the Chosen into a prison. Seeing the soldiers and the door, Charla knew they had arrived at their destination. It was now or never. The others were about to be locked up, and it was probably best that she not be locked up with them.

With one hand holding onto the edge of the pocket, Charla reached for her knife. It was a struggle to get it out and hold it while keeping herself from falling one way or the other. Of the two options, she preferred landing inside Ben's pocket, but that meant ending up inside a cell. She

finally got the knife free. She hoped it wouldn't hurt him too much as she drew her hand back and plunged it into Ben. There was no response. The blade had not gone all the way through the fabric. She jabbed her knife back toward Ben again with her full force. She needed to prick his skin, so he knew to take a fall, but only the tip of the tiny knife went through. It wasn't enough to send a message. She pulled it back and started to climb toward the waistband and the bare skin hidden by his shirt. Shirt fabric would be easier to get the blade through than jean fabric. She didn't get very far before she lost her grip on the knife. As soon as it left her hand, it started to grow. By the time it hit the ground, it was full size. Charla wondered how she could send Ben a message now.

"I thought you checked him for weapons?" a man asked the guard holding the rod attached to Ben.

"I did, and I swear he didn't have a knife on him."

"He must have."

The guard jerked Ben forward. "Where were you hiding that knife?"

Ben stumbled forward and fell to his knees.

"What do you think you're doing?" the guard shouted. Charla heard the sound of something heavy hitting flesh just before Ben screamed and fell face down on the floor. As he fell, she feared being squashed, but there was space between Ben's pocket and the floor. She dropped down just before the guard yanked the hood off of Ben's head, then grabbed his arms and roughly pulled him back up to stand on his feet. She wondered if Ben had fallen on purpose or if it had been the clumsy response to being pulled forward that it looked like.

She hoped no one was looking as she enlarged herself enough to be able to climb onto the shoe of one of the guards. As soon as she was in a place where she could hold on, she shrank down in size.

Every time the guard's foot lifted off the ground and swung forward, it frightened her. She bit her lip to keep from crying out. She was grateful when they stopped outside the first cell. She watched as a guard placed a coded card in front of the lock. Once the cell door opened, a guard pushed Allison in. They went on to a second cell. She was sitting on the jail guard's foot when he lifted it and kicked Ben in the back. The kick carried her briefly into the cell. As soon as she crossed the threshold of the door, she started to grow without wanting to or intending to. She was terrified of being seen and would have been if the guard's foot had spent any longer inside the cell than it did. It was clear that there was something about the jail cells that prevented the Chosen from using their gifts. Trevor was pushed into the same cell as Ben when his restraints and hood were removed.

The guards walked back out through the door to the place where Ben had fallen. Charla slid off the foot she was riding and sprinted across the floor to hide behind the leg of the desk standing near the door.

9. Into the Dark

Ben's neck hurt, and he was disappointed in himself. He had the gift of shrinking; why hadn't he used it? He could have stayed free to help the others. Now everything depended on Charla. Ben couldn't believe she had the good sense to shrink when he did not. He didn't trust her not to do something truly crazy and wished he'd stayed free to keep her on the right track. He could have if he had only thought to come through the portal shrunken in size as Charla had.

When the knife appeared out of nowhere, Ben knew it belonged to Charla. He guessed it was what she planned to poke him with. Ben pretended to stumble so he could fall to his knees. The blow to his shoulder was not a surprise, but it hurt far more than Ben expected. However, it was worth it if it got Charla to the ground without her breaking something.

Ben's hope of having Allison take away the pain disappeared when the soldiers pushed her into a cell and closed the door behind her, leaving him and Trevor on the outside. They passed a couple more cells before commanded to halt. Ben was freed from his restraints and kicked into the prison cell, where he fell to his knees. He was glad it was dark, so Trevor couldn't see the tears that sprang to his eyes.

Someone coughed, and Ben realized they were not the cell's only occupants.

"Who's there?" Trevor asked.

"There are ten of us in a cell meant to hold four," a voice said. "My name's Jupe."

"I'm Pok," another voice said.

"Peldo."

"Lou."

The other men called out their names one at a time.

"I'm Trevor and my friend's, Ben."

Ben clenched his fists at the use of the word friend. He didn't believe for one moment that Trevor thought of him as a friend.

"Have you come from the Guardian?"

"You know of the Guardian?" Trevor asked in surprise.

"Yes, some of us are, or at least we were Chosen of the Guardian. We were in training for work on other worlds. We are from the last few classes before the Watcher went rogue. All the Chosen sent so far are dead or in prison with us. It's been three years now, and we have just about given up all hope."

"It seems the Guardian still has hope," Trevor said. "Otherwise, we wouldn't be here now."

"Grek has done so much damage to our world that it will take a long time to reverse it," another voice said. "It's getting harder and harder to believe things will ever return to normal, and we'll get to finish our training."

"We've certainly had a firsthand demonstration as to why the work we do as Chosen is so important. Once evil is firmly in control, there is no justice, and peace is soon lost," Jupe said.

Ben gasped in pain as he stood up.

"Are you okay?" Jupe asked.

"I'm fine," Ben lied, his voice shaking.

"My friend's not telling the truth," Trevor said. "One of the guards clubbed him, and he's in pain."

Trevor's words left Ben with conflicted emotion. He was glad the others knew he had been clubbed and had a good reason for sounding shaky, but he was also annoyed that Trevor was speaking for him again.

"We've been hoping and praying for the Guardian to send someone to get us out of here," Pok said. "We thought it should be easy as this used to be the school for the Chosen. This is where off-worlders arrive, but Grek has found some way to neutralize their gifts and keep them imprisoned."

"We must escape from here," Jupe said. "They have been torturing us to try to find the Resistance headquarters. It's only a matter of time before someone who knows breaks."

"These off-worlders must have some very incredible gifts to have any hope of rescuing us from here," Peldo said.

"What gifts do you have?" Pok asked.

"Trevor and I were both…" Ben began but stopped speaking when Trevor poked him in the ribs. Ben swung at Trevor but missed him in the darkness and hit the side of the prison wall with his fist instead. The poke and the attempted punch left Ben reeling in pain. He'd think twice before he did that again. Then Ben realized that he had overreacted big time. What was he doing trying to punch Trevor? If his fist had connected, he might have done some serious damage. He had to get a grip if he was going to do his part to make this mission a success.

"—given the ability to turn into the last animal we saw." Trevor finished Ben's sentence but not in the way Ben would have. Ben didn't understand why he just didn't tell them the truth.

"That doesn't sound like a very useful gift to me," Pok said. "I can't imagine how you could use that gift to win against Grek."

"It could be useful," Trevor said. "The last animal Ben saw was a dragon. As long as he doesn't see something else, he can literally become a fire breathing dragon. I saw the dragon too, but unfortunately, after seeing the dragon, I saw a mouse. It's too bad this prison cell doesn't have bars instead of solid walls. I could slip through bars to the other side."

"You're not speaking the truth," Lou said. "There are no dragons anywhere near the school for the Chosen on Earth. Not only that, but I also don't believe the Guardian would give you such an unreliable gift. Not that it matters in this prison. You can't use your gifts as Chosen in these cells."

"I agree with Lou," Jupe said, "but perhaps it's wise to keep your gifts secret, for there are sometimes spies in prison with us. I don't think we have a spy in this cell, but…well, you never know. Not only that, but they could be listening to every word we say if there's a bug embedded in the walls or ceiling."

"We weren't given any clear guidance from the Guardian as to what to do once we got here," Ben said. "Do you have any suggestions as to what our first step should be?"

"If you get out of here," Lou groaned.

"The first thing you need to do is find the Resistance," Pok said.

"I don't think there's much of it left," Jupe said. "But what there is will be working on a plan to free all the prisoners. Most of the Chosen have been taken out of these cells and are in prison elsewhere. One of the things the Guardian will want you to do is rescue them."

Ben was about to say that they would do their best to rescue the Chosen and help the Resistance when Trevor jumped in and said what Ben had planned to say. He ground his teeth in irritation. The more time he spent with Trevor, the less he liked him. He told himself it had nothing to do with the fact that Allison was dating him, but everything to do with the fact that Trevor was a class A jerk. He also told himself it had nothing to do with what Miss Templeton had said to him before sending him to this world. Miss Templeton had told him that more than one Dragonborn lived with a lifetime of regret because of what they'd done in this season of their lives. She had called it Wrathborn and said if it were up to her, he would not be going off-world until he was safely through the hormonal changes that were part of it. She had likened it to puberty, but much worse.

Ben was confident he would hate Trevor even if he weren't starting to go through the changes that were part of being a Dragonborn of his age and gender. He felt resentment rise as he thought about Miss Templeton's words. What did she know about being Dragonborn? He was just fine. There was nothing wrong with him. The problem was Trevor.

The more Ben thought about it, the madder he got, but there was no heat in his belly for the first time in the last two years. He didn't have to struggle to keep flame from erupting, which was what he usually had to do when he was this angry. There wasn't even any smoke, and Trevor had made him angry enough that it should be surfacing. Actually, he should be struggling to keep flame from erupting. Was it possible that he couldn't even transform into a dragon in this prison cell?

Allison tramped down the fear that was threatening to overwhelm her when the door slammed shut, taking away the only source of light. Before that happened, she caught sight of at least a dozen frightened faces.

The pungent odor of unwashed bodies and overflowing latrines assaulted her nose and made her gag.

"Has the Guardian sent you?" a voice in the dark asked.

Allison was surprised to hear that the women in the cell knew about the Guardian. "Yes," she said.

"Allison, is that you? It's me, Zara. I met you when you came to Zargon. Is Ben here too?"

Allison didn't remember Zara's voice, but she'd met many people on Zargon, more than one who was named Zara. She turned in the direction the voice had come from. "Yes, Ben's here."

"Good," Zara said. "Has anyone else come?"

"My friend Trevor is with us."

"So, three of you came from Earth? Did anyone else come from another world?"

Allison hesitated. She was reluctant to say anything about Charla, but maybe she hadn't arrived yet. "I don't know," she finally said.

Allison heard the sound of someone struggling to breathe. "Is someone ill?" she asked.

"Yes, but there's nothing you can do," Zara said. "Your gift as a healer won't work here."

Allison moved toward the ragged breathing one slow step at a time. When her toe touched a body on the ground, she dropped to her knees and laid her hand on the woman in distress. Zara was right. Allison could not send that part of her carrying the Guardian's gift of healing into the woman's body to assess her. She found it deeply disturbing not to be able to call up her gift. It felt like she'd lost an essential part of who she was. Her whole identity had become wrapped up in being a healer. She couldn't imagine living a life without it.

Allison sat on the ground. She was unsure whether she wept for the woman near death or her lost gift as a healer. As she sat and cried, she held the dying woman's hand and stroked her forehead so she would know she wasn't alone.

10. Charla the Wizard

One of the guards stood by the cell door. He was an attractive man of about thirty with ash-blond hair. The only thing that distracted from his good looks was the scar that ran down from his left ear across his cheek to the corner of his mouth. The other man was older, perhaps in his late fifties. His dark hair peppered with grey. He was overweight and sat on a chair by the desk Charla was hiding behind. She listened to them talk and found it hard to contain her anger when they spoke about wanting to get the girl who'd just arrived in a cell by herself. She knew they were talking about Ben's friend Allison and was horrified by what they were saying.

"There are advantages to being on the night shift," Scarface said to the chubby man. "Fewer eyes around."

"Tonight, there are even fewer eyes than normal," the chubby guard responded.

"Those guys should have known better than to eat stew Sterna brought in," Scarface said.

"Good thing you and I were smart enough to turn it down."

"Someone should investigate whether he's working for the Resistance."

"If he was, I think he'd be smart enough not to eat it himself. Sterna is off sick, too."

"Are you sure he ate it?"

"Yes, I saw him. He ate the same thing that made more than half the guards sick."

"It's a good thing the Resistance doesn't know we're so short of guards tonight."

This is the best night for an escape, Charla thought. *But what can I do to make it happen?*

She knew she couldn't remain the size of a housefly if she were going to free the prisoners. The cards the guards had hanging on chains around their necks opened prison doors. She needed to get her hands on one of them.

Like the others, she had the gift of being a wizard, but she didn't want to use that gift for the first time when the cost of failure was so high. Any hope they had would be lost if she ended up in prison with the others because she didn't know what to do with her gift. She needed a place where she could practice controlling fire and wind and whatever other gifts came along with being a wizard.

She noticed there was a gap where the wall met the floor. She wondered what was behind it and whether there would be a place to practice without being seen. She was too tall to walk between the bottom of the wall and the floor, so Charla got down on her hands and knees and crawled. The dust she disturbed caused her to sneeze.

"Did you hear that?" Scarface asked.

"I didn't hear anything," the chubby guard responded.

Just as she suspected, there was a gap between two walls with enough light coming from under the wall that she could see what was on the floor. It was clean except for what looked like mouse droppings and some nails Charla guessed had been left there from the construction of the newly built wall.

She put her hands in front of her and called forth fire. She squealed in fear and excitement when a ball of fire appeared in her hands. She quickly cast it away, and it fell to the ground close to a curious mouse.

The mouse terrified Charla. It was much bigger than she was, and it frightened her to think it might see her as a food group. She was about to crawl back under the wall but then thought about how vulnerable that would make her. The mouse could grab her from behind. She grew in size instead. She became as big as the space between the two walls allowed. She formed another fireball. In its light, she could see that the mouse was still there. Its nose was twitching, and it was creeping closer. She threw the fireball in her hand toward it, and it turned and ran. The fireball fizzled and went out. She called forth more and threw them a dozen more times, becoming more accurate with every throw.

When she stopped forming fireballs, she noticed that four of them had not gone out. They had found a source of fuel and were continuing to burn. She ran to the first one and stamped it out with her foot. It had started in some sawdust. When she ran to the second one, the flame was taller than she was. She tried to call forth rain, but that wizard gift did not work well inside a building. All she managed to do was call forth a wind that caused the flame to grow. Charla knew she had no choice but to try to rescue the prisoners right now. They were at risk of burning if she did not get them out of their cells. She crawled back underneath the wall to where the guards were.

"Do you smell that?" the chubby man asked.

"It smells like something's burning," responded Scarface. "I'll go look in the cells and see if someone has managed to start a fire."

Once Scarface was gone, Charla grew to her standard size and threw a fireball at the chubby guard. He screamed as his clothing caught fire, immediately fell to the ground, and started rolling back and forth to put out the flame. Scarface heard the screams and came running back with his gun in his hand. He paused a second too long before pulling the trigger. Charla sent a fireball toward him, then dodged the energy beam he sent her way. Scarface ran to the wall near the hallway. There was an alarm attached to the wall that he wanted to push. Charla hit it with a fireball. When Scarface turned toward her, she hit him square in the chest. He took two steps and fell to the ground, where he rolled back and forth, trying to put out the fire.

Charla needed one of the cards the guards had around their necks to open the prison doors. Scarface's card was damaged beyond usefulness. She ran to the chubby guard and, while the flames were still burning, reached out to grab the card and pull it from his neck. She had it in her hand when the guard reached out and grabbed her arm. He raised his weapon in his other hand and squeezed the trigger. Charla threw herself sideways on top of the hand that was holding her, and the shot missed. The hold he had on her arm broke as she fell on top of it. She jumped up, pulled the gun away from the guard with one hand, and grabbed the card with the other.

While Charla struggled with the chubby guard, Scarface crawled to the wall where he managed to stand up and with blistered hands, push the bell he had tried to get to earlier.

Charla's fireball hadn't damaged it, and the alarm sounded.

It was ringing in Charla's ears as she used the coded card to go through the door to the prison cells. Scarface came stumbling after her. Charla ran directly to the prison cell that held Ben. She managed to open the cell door moments before Scarface caught up to her. The guard stood and looked at the men for a moment before realizing he was outnumbered. He turned and ran.

"Charla!" Ben exclaimed.

"The very same. I don't know what you'd do without me. Who manages to rescue you when I'm not around?"

"How did you—" Ben started, but Charla turned and ran to the next prison cell and opened the door. She ran from one cell to another. After every door was open, she yelled. "Fire. You need to get out of here fast." By then, the smell of smoke was strong, and people were coughing. They didn't need her to tell them they had to flee. The stream of people leaving the cells carried Charla along with them. When they went through the guard room, it was empty. Both of the soldiers had disappeared. Charla was relieved she hadn't killed them.

Alarms rang as the prisoners ran out. Charla used the stolen card to get them through the first two locked doors they came to, but it did not work when they arrived at the final door. The door could only be opened by someone whose eye was recognized by a retinal scanner.

They were milling around wondering what to do next when three guards showed up in full body armor carrying large weapons.

"Put your hands on top of your heads and sit on the ground," one of the guards ordered. "The fire will be out soon, and you will return to your cells."

Ben pushed himself to the front and transformed into a dragon. He didn't know what kind of weapons they had, but he would be better able to survive them as a dragon. His dragon body would provide shelter for the others should the guards shoot their guns. Two other Dragonborn must have come to the same conclusion, for they pushed their way to the front as well and transformed into dragons. The guards fired their weapons, and the dragons blasted them with fire. Neither the humans nor the dragons were severely hurt. The guard's special battle armor protected them. However, the dragon fire made them close their eyes and stumble backward away from the flame. Ben, Zara, and the third dragon, whose name Ben didn't know, grabbed the guns out of the guard's hands.

"Bring one of the guards here," Jupe commanded.

A couple of former prisoners grabbed one of the guards and brought him to Jupe, who tore off his faceplate and held him close to the scanner so his eye was in line with it. The door did not open.

Ben turned toward the other two guards. One had a different uniform than the other two. Ben grabbed him and brought him forward. The guard turned his head away, but Jupe grabbed his head and forced him to face the scanner. When he closed his eyes, Ben pulled open an eyelid and held it until the heavy door swung open.

When they stepped outside, they were in an open space surrounded by a high wall built of stone with a metal gate in the middle. On the walls, two sentries stood guard. At the moment, their attention was focused on the world beyond Truehaven. Between the wall with its sentries and the school, now turned into a prison, were several parked hovercraft.

A few of the escaping prisoners were now armed thanks to weapons they had taken from the guards. Jupe sent four of them out to deal with the two guards. When they returned, the captured guards were tied up, and everyone else was led out into the courtyard.

Through the metal gate, the lights of a distant city could be seen. The outline of five combat helicopters on their way to the prison were visible in front of the city lights.

"Can you do something about those helicopters," Jupe asked the Dragonborn.

"We can try," Ben said. He was about to leap into the air when a voice he knew yelled, "Wait. Take me with you." It was Jared, the human boy he'd met on Lushaka.

"Hey, Jared," Ben said, perplexed as to why he wanted to come.

"Good idea." Jupe pointed to objects that were flying off to the side of the helicopters. "He can focus on destroying the spy drones coming in with the helicopters. Peldo, give him the gun you have."

"He doesn't need a gun," Trevor said. He lifted his hand and pointed at a drone flying over the prison walls. A firebolt hit the drone and sent it crashing to the ground.

"Good job," Jupe said. "We don't want any of those things left to follow us into the city."

Trevor asked Zara's permission to be her rider. Zara crouched down to make it easier for him to climb up. Charla climbed on the third dragon. Soon all three Dragonborn were in the air.

Dragonfire proved ineffective against the armed combat helicopters. However, dragonfire and a bolt of a wizard's electrostatic energy proved to be very effective. Trevor was particularly good at calling the energy in the environment to himself and using it as a weapon. He and Zara were responsible for bringing down the first two helicopters. The wing of the dragon Charla rode was wounded, so he returned to the prison parking lot. By then, Charla had used her wizard gift to bring down several drones. Jared hit the third helicopter with a bolt of lightning in just the right spot and it went down. Jared, Trevor, and Charla demonstrated how effective a wizard was when riding a dragon into battle.

As maneuverable as the helicopters were, they could not compare with dragons on the wing. Ben managed to get behind one and grab it just above the tail rotor. It was a dangerous maneuver, but he managed to get hold of it in just the right spot. Ben swung it around in a circle. When he let it go, it spun out of control and hit a fifth helicopter, and they both went down in flames.

When the sky was free of drones, Ben noticed that Truehaven, the school for the Chosen, now turned into a prison, was built onto the side of a mountain. The walls that surrounded the school went three-quarters of the way around and ended at the mountain. As he landed in the courtyard, several small hovercraft lifted from the ground. They were crammed with people. Each of the cars, meant to carry no more than six had at least ten people. Several of them had someone standing on a back bumper holding onto ropes threaded through open windows.

"I need you Dragonborn to protect the hovercraft," Jupe said when they returned. "They don't carry weapons. Do you think you could do that and take two riders as well?"

"No problem," Ben said. Jupe joined Jared on his back. Allison had healed the third dragon, and he was able to fly with the other two.

They had almost reached the city when several drones flew toward them from the North. Ben assumed they were spy drones until the one closest to them opened fire. He climbed into the air to protect the riders on his back. Ben breathed deep and sent a long stream of flame at the drones, but they flew through them unharmed. He breathed deeply again and sent another long stream of flame in their direction. This time, a couple of them exploded. The weapons they carried were ignited by the heat of the dragonfire. Soon all of them were destroyed. Not long after that, the cars reached the outskirts of the city.

Ben kept an eye on the car Allison was in and followed it when the vehicles started to split up. Her car landed in a parking lot already scattered with hovercraft, and Ben followed it to the ground. The other dragons followed him.

Ben's riders climbed down, and he transformed back into a human. Jupe led them to a people mover, unlike anything Ben had seen before. It was attached to an overhead rail. Each car had twelve back-to-back chairs, six facing each direction. There were four cars waiting for passengers. He, Charla, Trevor, Allison, Zara, and Zane, a male Dragonborn of about forty, followed Jupe into the first car. Peldo and Lou joined them, as did an attractive blonde woman in her thirties. As soon as every seat was full, Jupe pushed a button, and a plastic cover came down to seal them in. Jupe then chose one of a group of four buttons. Ben assumed that each of the buttons represented a destination. The car slowly started moving forward as it steadily climbed upward until it was about twenty feet off the ground. It picked up speed when it finished climbing, and they soon left the industrial area behind and were traveling overtop residential streets and the occasional park. Ben could see other tracks with sky cars on them in every direction he looked. It appeared like there was a spider's web hanging over the city.

"Why didn't we just stay in the hovercraft?" Allison asked.

"Grek's soldiers are the only ones to use them in the city," Jupe said. "We would have been asked for an authorization number and shot down when we couldn't provide it."

11. Kiss Me Quick

When the people mover stopped, the attractive blond woman surprised Ben by grabbing his arm. She pulled him over to where Zara and Zane were. "The three of you are to come with me," she said.

Ben noticed Allison and Trevor going off with Jupe and a woman he didn't know from another car. They were going in a different direction than the woman was taking him. Peldo had Charla by the arm and was leading her away along with another couple. Ben stopped walking. "Wait! Where are you taking me? I should stay with the others from Earth."

"Sh!" the woman said. "Don't worry. We'll all end up in the same place. We can't all go the same way, or it will draw too much attention to us. It's safer if we go in twos and threes. And please keep your voice down. This whole city is crawling with drones. They watch and listen for unusual things."

Ben looked around to see if he could see one. At first, Ben didn't see any. Finally, he noticed one sitting not far away on the branch of a tree. Then he noticed several more.

"We need to avoid attracting their attention," the woman continued. "You can't ever let a drone see your eyes. The eyes of almost everyone in this world are in a database. If a drone decides to check you out and can't find a match, then reinforcements will come faster than you can say Dion Holkenstone, which is my name, by the way. Even if you don't do anything unusual, they may stop in front of you to do a scan just because they've got nothing better to do. You can't just close your eyes because their program tells them you are likely an enemy if you do. The drones will wait until you open them again, and if it takes too long, they call for human reinforcements."

"What can we do then?" Zara asked. "It sounds like they'll stop us before we get very far."

"We have discovered one thing that will make them go away without seeing our eyes." She paused and smirked. "They are programmed to view kissing as normal human behavior. So, if you see a drone, grab the person next to you and start kissing. Don't worry if you like them or their breath stinks. You don't stop kissing until the drone goes away."

"You're not serious," Zara said a little too loudly.

"I am. Zane and I will travel together. Let us get about a half-block away before you and Ben follow us." Dion started walking away but then turned around. "Make sure to close your eyes when you kiss."

Zara and Ben stood in awkward silence as they watched the other two walking away. Dion had taken Zane's arm, so they looked like a couple in love. When they were far enough away, Zara reached out and grabbed Ben's hand, and they started walking.

They hadn't gone very far when a screen on the side of a building came to life. There was another one about a block away, and when they looked up the street, they saw several more. The same thing appeared on every screen. Words were scrolling across them.

One of the gifts always given to Chosen when they leave their own planet is the gift of being able to understand the languages of the worlds to which they are sent. It was not a surprise to Ben when the words on the screen first appeared to be nonsense and then sorted themselves out as English.

A man was announcing the jailbreak and warning people not to harbor any of the escapees. Anyone caught doing so would face prison and maybe even death. He urged them to report anything strange they saw on the streets. If they saw strangers in their neighborhood, they were to report them to the block monitor. Anyone providing information that led to the recapture of the escaped criminals would receive extra rations. Pictures of the fugitives would soon be available. Dion started to walk faster after the last line appeared.

As they moved down the street, the same message replayed itself over and over again, one screen after another.

They had walked about three blocks when a drone flew down from a tree. It checked out the eyes of two women walking in the opposite direction and then flew over to

check out Dion and Zane's eyes. They kissed, and the drone eventually left without an eye scan. It flew directly toward Ben and Zara. When it got close, Zara stopped walking and stepped in front of Ben. When she pressed her body against his, Ben made an involuntary step back.

"Hold still. I won't bite," Zara whispered.

Her lips were warm and soft as they met his. For a few seconds, he stared at her with his eyes wide open. The drone was getting close enough to do a scan when he finally shut them.

At first, he was more aware of the sound of the drone buzzing in his ears and the breeze from its small rotors ruffling his hair than he was of the lips pressed against his. Then the kiss became more insistent, and the drone faded in the background to be replaced by the pounding of his heart. He could feel his ears growing warm and knew they had turned red. He hoped the blush would subside before Zara opened her eyes, but when he peeked through the slits of his eyelids, he saw that she was peeking out her own eye slits. She already knew he was blushing.

Ben's arms were hanging stiffly by his side until he
realized how odd that would look to anyone witnessing the
kiss. It would look like it was just something he was
enduring until it was over. He lifted his right hand and
brushed Zara's hair back from her face and then wrapped
both his arms around her and pulled her even closer than
she already was. The kiss became more passionate, and it
took Ben's breath away. He didn't notice that the drone had
flown away until Zara broke out of his arms.

"Was that your first kiss?" Zara asked.

"Of…of course not," Ben stuttered.

It worried him that Zara thought this was his first kiss.
Was he really that bad at it? He hoped Zara wouldn't ask
him when he had last kissed a girl. His first kiss had been a
disaster. He had tried to kiss Allison when she wasn't
interested. Later on, Allison had kissed Ben, but it was only
to make her boyfriend jealous, and the kiss was so short
that there was no time for Ben to kiss her back. As he
thought about it, he decided this felt like his first real kiss.
He wondered when he would be kissed like that again and
by whom.

They walked another three blocks before turning a
corner onto a busy street filled with tiny shops and
restaurants. Zara found the dress shops somewhat boring.
They all displayed the same plain brown and grey clothing

that the people on the street wore. Didn't people of Mellish ever go to a party where they dressed up in fancy clothes?

Dion and Zane were sitting on a bench in a park where children were playing, and lovers walked hand in hand. Dion waved them over. "The authorities expect to see larger groups of people here," she whispered to the other three.

Dion and Zane stood and walked through the park with Zara and Ben a few steps behind them. Zara stopped walking as they passed a food cart. The smells were incredible and reminded her of how hungry she was. She watched as a man ordered some food. After he ordered it, he moved in front of a scanner so that it could read his right eye. No money changed hands.

"What happens when you've escaped from prison or been identified as a resister?" Zara asked Dion quietly when they caught up to her. "How do you buy things?"

"You can't buy or sell anything on this world without an eye scan," Dion whispered. "If I tried to get something from that vendor, every drone from blocks around would converge on us, and it wouldn't take long before Grek's soldiers arrived and arrested me."

"How do you get food and pay for what you need then?" Zane asked quietly.

"You don't pay for it as you do on other worlds. Everyone earns credits from their jobs that are transferred from your account to a vendor's account with an eye scan,

so none of us can buy something. Me, because I'm a felon, and you, because your eyes are not in the system, " Dion said quietly. Then she spoke out loud so the vendor and his customers, as well as any nearby drones, could hear her.

"You'll see for yourself. I can make food as good as any you can buy from a street vendor. My place is only two blocks away. Come on, sweetie, let me show you where it is." Dion giggled and pulled Zane away.

The street vendor scowled at her.

"This, I've got to see for myself," Zane said loudly. Ben and Zara waited a few seconds and then followed them down the street.

As they moved out of the park, Ben noticed Dion nod to a man with a booth that said, "Life goes better with Luka Beans." The man nodded back, before pulling on the brim of his hat, which had the same slogan on it.

"What's he selling?" Ben asked.

"A frozen dessert made of luka beans," Dion said.

"He doesn't seem to have many clients," Ben observed.

"It's an acquired taste," Dion laughed. "I love it, but not many do. The beans are distilled and take on a much more robust flavor that most people find unpleasant."

They walked past many small shops before turning down an alley where they soon came to a dead end. A high fence blocked their way forward. On the left was a door painted green.

"Do you see any drones other than the one above the door?" Dion whispered. Zara and the other two scanned the nearby buildings but saw nothing.

"What about the one on top of the door?" Zara asked.

"It's a decoy. The guts are missing, so it doesn't send any images back, but if another drone comes down the alley and sees it, it will normally leave because its program tells it the area is already under surveillance."

Zara felt some sense of disappointment that the drone in the alley would not fly down and try to scan their eyes. She'd been looking forward to kissing Ben again. He was a hero on Zargon for his part in defeating the rogue Dragonborn, Zork, and for rescuing the king from the world of Farne. Many a girl on Zargon had a crush on Ben without ever having met him. She couldn't wait to tell her friends that she had kissed him.

12. Peefall

Dion stepped forward after one last look around and pulled out a retinal scanner folded up against the door frame. As soon as the door opened, she ushered the others inside. When Dion closed the door, they stood in the dark until she found a light switch. They were at the top of a flight of concrete steps leading down into a basement. An unpleasant smell of mildew and decay grew stronger with each step down they took.

Long-forgotten furniture and some rolls of stained carpet littered the space. Dion pulled these aside to reveal a grate in the floor. Pulling the grate away, she motioned for the others to climb down a rusty metal ladder.

A nasty smell rose from whatever was under the basement, and Ben shuddered as he climbed down the ladder into the darkness below. When he reached the bottom, he heard the sound of skittering and caught movement on the edges of the faint light that shone from above. He watched as Dion stepped onto the ladder. She moved the grate back over the hole and then pulled a rope. The light disappeared almost entirely after the carpet moved back in place.

The smell in the tunnel reminded Ben of outhouses. He was embarrassed to discover he was shivering. It was cool, but he was honest enough with himself to recognize it for what it was. His fear made him angry. He was Dragonborn, for crying out loud. What could be down here that could take on a dragon? Maybe nothing, but he would not be able to transform in this small space surrounded by concrete, rock, dirt, and who knows what else. Whatever dangers there were, he would have to face them as a human.

He didn't trust himself to speak, so he waited in the dark for Dion to tell them what to do. He heard her moving about, and then there was light. She had a small flashlight in her hand. She turned it on and handed it to Ben before reaching into a crack in the wall and pulling out three more flashlights. She used the one she kept for herself to find a switch on the side of the ladder. She turned the light in the basement above them off, and the faint glimmer from above disappeared. She walked over to a corner, knelt, and reached inside a roll of rusted metal that had been discarded years ago. She pulled out four good quality raincoats and four pairs of oversized boots. She put one of the raincoats on and put her feet, still wearing shoes, into the boots. She used a strap to tighten the boots around her ankle.

When everyone had their raincoat and boots on, she pulled out some plastic gloves and handed them out. "Don't touch anything, and don't let anything touch you if you can avoid it. Don't step in water puddles unless I tell you it's okay. Some of those puddles are deeper than they look, and many are filled with a toxic soup. Step in one, and it might be the last thing you do." Dion reached back inside the roll of rusted metal and pulled out goggles. "Put these on to protect your eyes, and don't think about getting your hands anywhere near your face."

"Aren't there better ways of getting where we're going?" Ben asked.

"There might be, but this is the only way in that I know. Most members of the Resistance only know one way. If this route is compromised, it will be destroyed, and I will be assigned to a different tunnel.

"You mean you're the only one who comes in this way?" Ben asked puzzled.

"No, usually, there are a dozen people or more for every entrance."

"How do you know it's not compromised?"

"I don't, but every route is electronically monitored. The people using them must be accompanied by someone whose eyes are on record as belonging to that entrance. Otherwise, an alarm rings at Resistance headquarters." To illustrate, she pulled a scanner from where it was hidden behind the ladder and placed it in front of her right eye.

"Follow me," she said quietly.

Dion pulled the hood of her raincoat over her head and walked bent over into the tunnel. Ben and the others followed her example. The boots were hard to walk in, and Ben found that the best he could do was shuffle. His flashlight revealed a rough pathway between two drainage ditches filled with a putrid liquid. Water or some other liquid was dripping from the ceiling. They hadn't walked

far when the beam of Ben's flashlight shone in the lifeless

eyes of a dead creature resembling a rat. A little further on,

there was a chemical smell that made Ben's eyes water. He

started coughing and didn't stop until the smell diminished.

"What was that?" he asked loudly.

"Sh," Dion responded in a loud whisper. "I have no

idea," she said more quietly. "Someone above us has

broken sewage pipes. Perhaps because they have been

putting stuff they shouldn't down their drain. The sewage

system we're in was abandoned a long time ago. A new one

was built above us. Most people have forgotten this one

exists, which works out well for the Resistance."

"Living down here can't be healthy," Ben said.

"It's healthier than living where Grek can get his hands

on us. Now be quiet. You never know where the new pipes

are. If they are touching this one, they might conduct

sound. The odd person mentions now and then how they

sometimes hear voices coming from the ground, so we

travel through them as silently as we can."

Ben followed Dion without speaking after that. He was

glad when the chemical smell faded, but it was replaced by

the smell of stale urine. Ben had become familiar with the

odor his first year at Fairhaven. He had forgotten to flush

the toilet when he left to go to school for the first time. Neither Ben nor his dad had returned to the house for months. The smell, when they did return, was terrible, but it was better than the stench in the tunnel he was in now.

As they walked, the smell grew more potent, and it was making Ben gag. He could hear the sound of water falling somewhere in front of them. The awful smell was all he could think about, and he ran into Dion when she stopped walking.

"Watch where you're going," she said. "We've got to go through there. Keep your back to the left wall where there's a ledge. The waterfall has made that puddle deeper than it looks. Go through the middle, and that stuff will come up over the top of your boots."

"What is it?" Ben asked quietly.

"What does it smell like to you?" Dion asked.

"You've gotta be kidding. We're going to be showered with urine."

"That's why you're wearing a raincoat." Dion turned sideways and started sliding along the left wall of the tunnel. "There must be a large apartment complex above here because there's always a waterfall in this spot."

"You mean a peefall, don't you?" Zara asked, laughing.

Dion and Zane laughed, but Ben didn't see it as being very funny.

Ben watched Dion and then Zara walk safely across before following their example. He was grossed out when a stray drop hit his cheek. He lifted his hand to brush it away but stopped when he noticed several drops on the plastic gloves he was wearing. They were closer to the splashback and were wet with urine.

"We've only got one more dangerous spot to cross, and then we're home free," Dion whispered.

She walked a short distance before stopping at a spot where two seven-foot planks rested against the wall. "Can you take the other end?" she asked, preparing to pick up one end herself.

"Let Zane and I take that," Zara said as she took the wooden plank out of Dion's hands. "Do we need the other one?" Ben asked.

"All we need is one," Dion said. "We always need to make sure there is at least one plank on both sides. The next person who comes will need to make sure to bring one back across before they move on."

Zara and Zane carried the wooden plank for several yards and stopped when they came to a place where water flooded across the tunnel floor. Dion took the end of the two-by-four from Zara and slid it across the pool. She then stepped on it and used it to cross to the other side. She turned and gestured for the others to follow. Then Dion asked Zane and Ben to pick up the plank and carry it to higher ground. They dropped it beside two more planks that rested against the wall.

"We try to keep the planks from getting covered in

slime, which would make them slippery. The water doesn't

reach this spot."

Dion stopped walking when they reached a dead end. She gave her flashlight to Ben and pulled on a lever near the wall. A valve opened above her, and water flowed down. Dion stood underneath the flow until her raincoat and boots were clean. She rubbed her hands with the gloves still on under the water to make sure she got everything off them. She then took the flashlights from Ben and invited him to stand beneath the flow of water and clean himself. The other two did the same. She opened a door and walked up two steps to a landing.

"Close the door behind you," she said to the others,

speaking in a normal tone of voice. When everyone was through, Ben found a knob and pulled it to close the door. He then climbed the steps to where he had last seen Dion and found her at the end of a hallway chiseled through rock. Ben was quite sure that where they were now had never been part of the sewage system.

Dion removed her coat and boots, and the others followed suit. She opened a door, and Ben and the others found themselves in a large bright room filled with people. They had arrived at the Resistance headquarters.

13. Resistance Headquarters

They went to the dining hall, where they found Allison sitting at a long table. She was near the wall on the right side. Trevor was nowhere in sight, and Ben looked forward to having a private conversation with Allison. He'd almost reached her when he heard Charla calling his name. He decided to pretend he hadn't heard her because he didn't want to listen to Charla brag about saving his life again, but she was not willing to be ignored. When Ben did not answer, Charla launched herself toward him and threw her arms around his neck. She kissed him on the lips and then hugged him. Ben was shocked. He never expected Charla to kiss him.

"My favorite person to rescue," Charla said loudly. "Who rescues you when I'm not around?"

Ben looked over Charla's shoulder at Allison. Her eyebrows raised in surprise. Ben's first thought was to let Allison know there was nothing between him and Charla, but then decided it might be better for her to think there was. She might look at him differently if she thought other girls were interested.

He tore his eyes away from Allison and smiled at Charla. Then he returned her kiss before stepping out of her embrace. He caught sight of Zara. The Dragonborn girl was frowning. He guessed she disapproved of the kiss because of the rule against getting romantically involved with people from other worlds. In what world did he belong? Was it Earth, or was it Zargon?

"Most of the time, I'm the one doing the rescuing," Ben said, his voice just as loud as Charla's had been. "Come and meet my friend," he added before Charla could recount for everyone how many times she had rescued him. He took Charla's arm and walked her over to where Allison sat.

After introductions, the ever-gracious Allison thanked Charla for rescuing all of them from prison as well as for saving Ben on several other occasions.

"Where's Trevor?" Ben asked.

"He's in a meeting with the leaders of the Resistance."

Ben couldn't help it. Some part of his brain told him he was unreasonable, but the smoke issuing from his mouth was accompanied by a small amount of flame. He hated the idea that Trevor was in a special meeting while he was not.

Allison stared at him in shock. "What's up with you?"

"We were all appointed by the Guardian. They should have waited and included all the Chosen in whatever meeting they are having." Ben didn't look at Allison when he said that.

"I agree with Ben," Charla said.

The fact that Charla agreed did not satisfy the part of Ben's brain that wondered if he was unreasonable.

"Sometimes decision making is easier without a large number of people involved," Dion said. She had come up behind Ben along with Zane and Zara. "Besides, many Chosen were already here when you arrived, so this is going to be different from your other trips off-world. You are all part of a large team rather than lone riders sent out to save the day."

The smoke coming forth from Ben diminished a bit. It subsided even more when he noticed that everyone was staring at him. Charla moved close to Dion and began to ask her questions. Ben took a couple of steps away in case Charla wanted privacy.

"I remember what life was like when I was your age," Zane said quietly in Ben's ear. "I felt the whole world was against me. Luckily, I wasn't sent off-world until it was over. It's hard to control your emotions when you're going through the Wrathborn season, but you need to, or they'll be a real problem, not just for you but for everyone around you. I'll do what I can to help, but the battle will be yours."

Zara had stepped close to Ben. "I'm surprised you were selected, but maybe they thought it wouldn't be so hard for you because you are part human." Her voice was quiet and full of sympathy.

"How long does it usually last?" Ben asked.

"Depends on the Dragonborn," Zane said. "For some, it's a matter of days. Others don't seem to make it to the other side. It took me six weeks."

"My brother was in it for three years," Zara said.

Ben looked at Zara in horror. The flame in his belly completely died out. The thought of struggling to control his emotions for three years terrified him.

Dion took Charla's arm and drew her close to Ben. "You'd like to know what's going on?" she said. "I understand that. I'll tell you what I can. The first thing we need to focus on is provisioning. We can't find a way to rescue the other Chosen and get the Guardian's Medallion if we don't have food. I'm told the Medallion's what's keeping him alive, and it must be true, for no one on this world lives to be over six hundred years old. Once we get the Medallion away from him, I understand it will choose a new Watcher."

"Technically, it's not the Medallion that chooses," Allison said. "It is the Guardian's spirit infusing the Medallion who does the choosing."

"If we get the Medallion away from Grek, then the Guardian will either send someone new through one of the portals or choose someone who is already here," Dion said. "Have any of you been identified as a future Watcher?"

Ben shot Allison a worried look. If any of them had, he thought it would be her. The last thing he wanted was for Allison to stay on this world. Ben relaxed when he saw that Allison was shaking her head. He let out a sigh of relief as he shook his head from side to side.

"None of the Dragonborn have been identified as possible replacements," Zara said. "Dragonborn are not good at power-sharing, so I doubt your new Watcher will be one of us. Most of ours come from worlds other than Zargon. Our new Watcher came from Earth with Ben. Mack is still a teenager, so it will be several hundred years before we need a new one if all goes well."

Ben thought about Mack and how the boy had followed him to Zargon against everyone's wishes. It turned out that the Guardian had a plan for the strange boy who had seemed so small and vulnerable. If the Guardian could turn Mack into a Watcher, then perhaps the Guardian could use any one of them.

"How's Mack doing?" he asked.

"He's doing well," Zara said.

"Watchers receive the memories of past Watchers, so it is not impossible to become one without being identified and trained in advance," Dion said. "Theoretically, any one of us could be the next Watcher on Mellish. Although it seems like the Guardian normally chooses someone from off-world."

"Lushaka's Watcher is a Mer from our own world," Charla said. "Perhaps because it would be hard for anyone other than a Mer to be a Watcher on a world almost entirely made up of water."

"As I said before, it's not likely to be a Dragonborn," Zane said. "We are too attracted to power and wealth. This world could be in worse trouble than it is now if one of us were the next Watcher."

Ben thought of the Watcher he'd met on Farne. He was a Dragonborn who had not been able to transform. He was stuck somewhere between human and dragon. Ben thought of Zachary as a lizard man.

"It's most likely to be a healer," Dion said. "We used to have two healers. One was murdered by Grek a year ago. The other is not likely to be chosen as the new Watcher because she is very old. None of us know where she is at the moment. Wherever she is, I hope she's training her replacement. I've asked the other groups if a healer came with them. They've all said no. As far as I know, Allison is the only healer to come from off-world. Perhaps she's been sent to be our new Watcher."

Ben was appalled by Dion's words. "No," he said without thinking.

Ignoring Ben, Dion turned to Allison. "Have you ever received a word directly from the Guardian?"

"I believe I have," Allison replied.

"Then it is possible you are this world's next Watcher," Dion said.

Ben turned and walked away. Charla tried to tag along, but he told her he wanted to be alone. He walked back inside the cave he had just come from and sat down with his back against the wall. The human part of him wanted to cry. The dragon part of him wanted to rage and burn everything in sight. Not that there was much that could ignite when you were underground and surrounded by rock.

He closed his eyes and tried to think of fishing and horseback riding and everything that brought him a deep sense of peace. One thought kept intruding. It settled his mind a little even though he knew the idea was unworthy of one of the Guardian's Chosen. *At least she won't end up married to Trevor if she's the Watcher of Mellish.*

14. Rescue Plans

Mara, the Resistance leader, turned out to be a short woman in her late forties with mousy brown hair. A scar sliced across her right cheek, and her ear was missing on that side. She had one mechanical arm that seemed to operate as well as the one made of flesh and blood.

"I'm so pleased you escaped," Mara said. "We had planned a rescue for tonight but called it off when we heard the alarms."

Charla remembered the conversation she'd overheard about food poisoning and guessed the guard who'd brought in the stew was part of the Resistance.

She also wondered what time it was. It must be long after midnight. Perhaps it was even morning by now. There was no way of telling when you were underground.

"We were trying to stockpile enough food to last us all seven days before staging a rescue. We didn't quite have enough when we decided not to wait any longer," Mara said. "The first thing we'll need to do is bring in more food. The donations do not provide enough for our needs. Since we can't buy food, we need to steal it. Now that's something I never thought to hear myself say as a Chosen of the Guardian, but then I never thought to see the day when the Watcher of Mellish would control all of the world's resources and use it to make himself and his few friends rich." Mara paused for a moment as if lost in thought. "I now call on Commander Jupe to tell us what our next step is."

Charla felt a moment of pride when Jupe stepped forward. He was one of the people she'd rescued. She barely stopped herself from pointing that out to the people standing beside her.

"We'll hit several distribution sites all at the same time," Jupe said. "We're sending out six teams with off-world Chosen on each one. Teams two, four, ten, fourteen, and twenty are up. If the leaders can stand, I'll assign your Chosen. In the next hour, I will meet with the leaders to explain the assignments."

Ben stood beside Charla, waiting for Mara to call his name. He didn't know whether to hope they were on the same team or not. Charla could do some crazy things, but she always managed to save the day in the end.

"Team two will have Zara and Jared join them." The leader of that group stood, so Zara and Jared could see who he was.

They were down to the last team. Ben, Trevor, Charla, and Allison were the only people not yet assigned.

"Allison will stay here so she can treat any team members who come back wounded," Jupe said.

Ben was relieved to hear that. It made sense to keep your healers behind and available for all the wounded when you had many fronts in your battle.

That meant he was on the last team with either Charla or Trevor and maybe both. What a nightmare! If he had his choice, he'd choose Charla over Trevor any day of the week.

"Trevor and Ben will be on team twenty," Jupe said.

Ben's heart sank. Next to him, Dion put up her hand. That was a surprise. Ben hadn't realized she was a team leader.

"The teams will be ready to leave two hours after our evening meal," Jupe continued.

"Wait," Charla called out. "You forgot about me."

Jupe ignored her and went on speaking.

The fact that Charla wasn't named didn't come as a complete surprise to Ben. *Wow*, he thought. *It didn't take Jupe long to figure out that Charla isn't a good team player.*

Ben looked at the Mergirl in sympathy. She would not take being left behind well. He wondered why the Guardian had sent her, then realized they might still be in prison without her. Maybe getting them out of prison was the only reason Charla came on this quest. Even if she wasn't put on a team, she had already proved her worth with just that one action.

To say Charla was unhappy would be an understatement. Mara and Jupe were heading into a meeting room when she stopped them. "Why did you leave me off a team?" Charla said, far too loudly. "I can stay transformed for a long time in all kinds of situations if that's what you're afraid of. I won't suddenly lose my legs and have a Mer tail like I used to. I've put in the practice needed to be the best Fairwaters has to offer."

"I'm sure you are one of the best Mer students at your school; otherwise, you wouldn't be here; however, the assignment the others are going on is not the best use of your gifts," Mara said soothingly.

Mara's tone of voice irritated Charla. It was like she was speaking to a petulant child.

"You can't expect me to stay here while the others go off on an adventure." Charla had to stop herself from stomping her foot.

Mara frowned at Charla, which made her scarred face look grotesque. "No one is going on an adventure. This is a flesh and blood struggle that might end up in the death of many fine people, including Chosen."

Charla was appalled at her own thoughtlessness. "Of course," she said. "I misspoke, but I was sent here by the Guardian. And I don't think it was so I could sit here and do nothing while the others go off and do something to save your world."

"We agree," Jupe said. "That's why we have a special mission only you can do. It's dangerous and requires courage, prudence, and wisdom for you to stay alive and keep the Resistance safe."

"It is clear you have courage, but I'm wondering whether you have prudence," Mara said.

Prudence, Charla thought. She only had a vague idea of what the word meant. Charla doubted Lea Waterborn, the Watcher of Lushaka, would ever use it to describe her. "I can be as prudent as anyone else if I need to be," she said, despite her doubts.

"We're going to take a chance you can be, for as you say, you have been sent here by the Guardian, and you have the needed gifts," Mara said.

"Shall we tell her now?" Jupe asked Mara.

"Come into the office with us." Mara gestured to a chair, and once Charla was seated, she continued speaking. "This is your mission if you choose to accept it. We want to send you into Grek's residence. He must touch the Medallion every day to keep from aging. Since he hardly ever leaves the palace, it must be in there somewhere. We need to know where he keeps it and how we can get people in and out of the palace. We also need to know where the rest of the imprisoned Chosen are."

"If you find the Medallion, we don't want you to try to bring it back on your own," Jupe said. "We've got one shot, and we want to make sure careful thought goes into every detail."

"Why are you sending just me?" Charla asked. "This sounds like an important mission."

"You are the only one who can safely get in. Grek's residence is so secure that it would be hard for a fly to find a way in without an invitation. But we were able to lay our hands on the building plans, which show a vulnerability Grek may not know about. And even if he knew, it would never cross his mind that someone could come in that way."

Mara unrolled a scroll in front of her to reveal a map. Charla and Jupe leaned forward to see.

"This circle here is a fountain," Mara said, pointing to a spot outside of the front door. "Inside, there is a smaller one." She pointed to a circle in the foyer of the lavish residence. "The two fountains are connected by a pipe that goes underground. We think you can enter the fountain on the outside of the building and travel through it to the one inside the palace."

"What do you think?" Jupe asked. "Is it something you can do?"

"It should be easy," Charla said.

"We're going to wait until tomorrow night to send you. Until then, you cannot say a word or even tell people you are going on a special mission. The fewer people who know, the better."

Charla's smile disappeared. Her first thought had been that she couldn't wait to tell Ben and Jared, but now she couldn't tell anyone. How aggravating when she wanted to tell the whole world about her special assignment. I guess this was one of those lessons in maturity Lea Waterborn put such high value on.

She tried not to let her disappointment show. "So just to be clear," she said. "You want me to find out where Grek has the Medallion, find out where the other Chosen are held captive, and you want me to find a way into the palace that non-Merfolk can use."

"It is a lot to ask," Mara said.

"I can do it if anyone can," Charla said, wanting to give the impression that she had no doubts even though she was full of them.

15. The Raid

As soon as the evening meal was over, Dion gathered her team members together at a table in the dining hall. She introduced Ben and Trevor to the two men and two women who were going with them. Jaks and Shank had never been arrested and could undergo a retinal scan without raising the kind of alarm that would bring tons of security down on them. Patrice was Shank's sister, and she too had never been arrested. Florrie's eyes would raise alarms. She was the daughter of the Resistance leader and had been in training as a Chosen. Dion decided that she would travel with Trevor, Jaks with Florrie, Ben with Patrice, and Shank would travel alone.

"Our mission is Distribution Centre Ten on the outskirts of the city," Dion began. "There may be increased surveillance because of its proximity to the prison, but it is the only place that has luka beans."

"This is an important mission then," Florrie said. "We are running very low on luka beans."

"Haven't we tried and failed to breach that location before?" Jaks asked.

"Yes," Dion replied, "but we've never had two wizards, one of whom has superpowers and the other who is Dragonborn with us before. We will take a people mover to the warehouse. Our information tells us that the trucks are loaded in the afternoon and make their deliveries the next morning. With any luck, we won't have to load them. Regardless, we will leave in those trucks with luka beans in them. Are there any questions?"

"Why are luka beans so important?" Ben asked.

"They're a food staple that provides all the vitamins and minerals a body needs to be healthy," Dion said. "You could eat nothing but luka beans and be just as healthy as someone eating the most varied and expensive diet. What makes the beans ideal is that they keep for a long time when dried and retain their nutritional value."

"You had some at supper," Florrie said.

"Were they the round things in the stew?" Ben asked.

"Yes, but some were also ground into flour and used to make the bread you ate," Florrie said. "We all take a turn in the kitchen. Today was my turn, so I have firsthand knowledge of how your food is made."

Ben wondered if he was expected to take a turn.

Dion reminded them that kissing was the best way to get a drone to move on without scanning your eyes.

The screens on the buildings showed Grek looking down from the sky as children played and adults walked hand in hand through the park. It showed a picture of good harvests and families sitting at tables with all kinds of good food in front of them. It was played on a loop, and there was a reminder to watch out for escaped prisoners between the repeats. They flashed pictures of some of the people they were looking for. Dion and Jupe's faces came up frequently.

Ben saw a good number of drones as they traveled, but none came to verify their identity. Ben was a bit disappointed not to have an excuse to kiss the attractive redhead he traveled with. He just about asked her if something was wrong. She seemed to have a stiff leg and refused to sit down when they were on the people mover.

They arrived earlier than the arranged rendezvous time because of their uneventful trip. A short time later, Dion came with Trevor, followed by Jaks and Florrie. Shank arrived just as Ben started to worry that something had happened to him.

"I want Shank, Jaks, Florrie, Patrice, and Ben at the front of the building," Dion said. "Trevor and I will go and see if he can use his super strength to make a back door into the warehouse. Florrie is in charge of the attack on the front of the building."

Florrie led them to a doorway with a truck parked in front of it. She and the others retrieved long guns hidden in their pant legs. Ben now knew why Patrice had walked so stiffly and had chosen not to sit when they rode the people mover. She pulled up the bottom of her shirt and retrieved an ammo belt. The others did the same. Soon, they all had fully loaded guns in their hands.

As they walked the remaining block to the warehouse, Ben noticed the number of drones increased. There were six flying back and forth in front of the door, and Ben could see several more roosting on windowsills and roofs. He noticed that three of the drones were larger than the others.

"Do those drones carry weapons?" Ben asked.

"Yes," Florrie said. "You mostly find them in industrial areas because they aren't great at judging between a thief in the night and children at play. Every year innocent people are killed when one of those things stumbles into a residential area."

"There were some weapon-carrying drones when we were coming into the city," Ben said. "They were bigger than these."

"What's the plan?" Shank asked when they reached the front of the warehouse.

"I want Ben to attack the front doors and make as much noise as he can while the rest of us destroy drones," Florrie said. She pushed past Ben to a place where her back would be against the wall and started firing. The others did the same. The six drones flying in front of the door soon lie broken on the ground. There were whirling sounds all around as nearby drones took to the air and flew toward them. Drones were coming from up and down the block.

The air was thick with them, and they were all converging on Ben and his companions. Some of the drones coming toward them carried weapons. The nearest ones were intent on getting close enough to scan their eyes.

Ben felt pain in his arm and touched it. When he looked at his hand, there was blood. He hadn't noticed the weaponized drone sitting on the roof until it rose into the air and shot him. Shank fired his gun, and his bullet sent it crashing to the ground.

"It's just a scratch," Florrie said to Ben after examining his arm. "You'll be fine. Forget about it and attack the door. We need to make this look like a real threat to the warehouse. We want the drones focused on what's happening here, so they ignore what's happening at the back."

Ben formed a fireball and threw it at the door. It wasn't very large and when it hit there was little sound. He formed another one. This one was larger but didn't create the drama Florrie was looking for. He wondered what else he could try, then remembered that a wizard could use the natural electrical charge in the world around them to generate lightning bolts. Ben reached out his hands and called electrostatic energy to himself. His whole body soon felt like it was ready to explode, so he reached out his right arm toward the door with his fingers outstretched. He felt the charge race through him, and then a lightning bolt hit the door with such force that there was an explosion of light and sound.

"That's the way to do it," Florrie said.

The door was damaged, and one of its hinges gave way. Drones flew toward them from every direction, including from inside the warehouse. Several of them carried weapons.

"Hit the door one more time," Florrie said. "Then help us get rid of drones."

Ben once again drew electrostatic energy from the sky and things around him. When his body felt like it couldn't take any more, he sent a lightning bolt into the doors. This time, one of the two large doors was ripped almost entirely from its hinges.

Florrie moved toward the door. "We've got about twenty minutes before human soldiers arrive in choppers. We need to get rid of all the drones so they can't track us when we make our escape."

More drones were flying in the air than Ben could count. He wondered how they could get rid of all of them in twenty minutes.

"Let's go," Florrie said, and she ran across to the warehouse and turned so her back was against the broken door. The two Mellish men, Patrice, and Ben followed her example. With their backs protected, they fired their weapons.

The drones were programmed to go toward suspicious action and noise, but they weren't programmed to do it stealthily. They did not hide even if there was something to hide behind. They did, however, move rapidly and erratically when under attack. Ben would form and throw a fireball only to discover the drone he was aiming at had moved. Most times, he still hit one because there were so many in the air. Twisted pieces of metal, rotors, and wires littered the ground, but there were still a few dozen either shooting at them or trying to get close enough to scan their eyes.

Ben decided it was time to try something new. He called up wind and sent it at the drones flying in front of them. The drones hit the building across the street, while he and the others hit the broken door behind them because of the backdraft. It gave way, and they ended up sprawled on the ground just inside the warehouse. When Ben opened his eyes, the last remaining drones lay crumpled on the ground in front of the warehouse across the street. The force of the wind had blown out the windows and doors of that warehouse, but the skies were empty.

"Warn us next time," Florrie said as she picked herself up from where she lay on top of the broken door. "Wish you would have done that earlier, though. I don't see any more active drones. Do you?"

"Who can see anything?" Shank asked, trying to rub dirt out of his eyes.

"Let's go further into the warehouse and see how the others are doing," Florrie said when everyone seemed to have recovered from the wind enough to see where they were going.

They stepped over the broken door, and Ben was amazed at the size of the warehouse. It was the length and width of a football field. At the other end, they could hear the sound of a battle. Dion and Trevor had gotten inside the warehouse but were under attack by weapon carrying drones.

"Come with me," Shank said as he climbed into the driver's seat of a forklift. "Let's finish this off so we can get out of here."

They all held on tight while Shank raced down to the other end of the warehouse. Dion and Trevor were hiding behind sacks that spilled luka beans through newly-shot holes. Several drones were down, but several more were still in the air.

Ben felt a sudden jolt in his back and was glad for the bulletproof vest the Resistance had loaned him. He turned and saw an armed drone about to fire on him again. Ben threw himself off the forklift while sending a ball of fire toward it. He hit it hard and it exploded. Soon all the drones lay broken on the ground.

"They were in here when we came," Dion said. "They must be how the government does security nowadays." She turned toward Trevor. "Go and finish ripping out the wall."

Ben wished the Guardian had given him the gift of super strength as he watched Trevor make a hole large enough to drive a truck through.

Dion opened the back door of a truck. "Good. It is full of luka beans. How about the others?"

Patrice and Jaks each checked out a truck. Both of them were full of beans.

"Time to get out of here. Soldiers will be here any minute." Dion climbed into the driver's seat of the truck she planned to drive. "Trevor, come with me. Jaks and Patrice will each drive a truck. Ben, I'd like you to fly above us as a dragon for the next several blocks with Shank on your back. Shank will help you bring down any drones that are following us. Try to destroy them so they can't follow the trucks. If you see any choppers, I want you to lead them away from us."

Dion started the truck, put it into gear, and drove it out the hole Trevor had made. The other two trucks followed.

When Ben walked out of the warehouse, he could hear the sound of helicopters closing in on it. They were coming from the west. Dion turned the trucks onto a road leading north. Ben watched them leave as he waited for the helicopters to arrive.

"What's your plan to get us out of here?" Shank asked.

"I thought you'd have a plan." Ben transformed into a dragon and crouched down so Shank could get on board. "Hold on," he said. "I'm going to fly straight up, so we are above the choppers. With any luck, they won't see us, and our attack will come as a surprise."

Ben's plan would have worked if it wasn't for a weapon carrying drone who was late in coming to find out what all the noise was. As Ben rose into the sky, it flew behind him and shot its weapon, catching Shank under the armpit in a spot not protected by his weapon proof vest. Ben heard Shank grunt and asked if he was okay.

"Fine," Shank said in a quiet voice that Ben could hardly hear. Ben looped around and breathed dragonfire at the drone. The ammunition it carried caught fire and exploded. The first helicopter had just arrived, and the drone fell into its rotors, causing it to crash. The remaining two helicopters started to climb so they could target Ben. He dropped from the sky on top of the closest helicopter and drove it into the one that was following. Both lost control and spiraled down to the ground, where they exploded in flames.

Ben was amazed. Not every battle was this easy. Wait until he told the others that he brought down three helicopters all on his own. That thought made him wonder about Shank. He wasn't entirely on his own, even though Shank had done nothing to help. "Are you okay?" he asked again.

"Not...okay," Shank said.

"What can I do?"

"Fly...building...red roof...four blocks...north."

Ben flew up into the air, saw the red roof, and dropped down into the street in front of it. The trucks had just arrived when he got there. He settled on the ground, and Shank fell from his back and lay by his feet. Ben transformed back into a human and dropped to his knees beside him.

The door of the garage opened, and more than a dozen people came out, gathering around Shank in concern

"Go, unload the trucks," Dion said. "We'll do what we can for Shank."

"What happened?" Patrice asked as she dropped to her knees.

"I think a drone shot him." Ben pointed to the blood seeping out from under Shank's arm.

Patrice put her hand on her brother's neck to check for a pulse. She held it there for a moment and then howled, "He's dead. My brother is dead." She leaned over Shank and rested her head on his shoulder while she cried. Dion checked his pulse, looked up at Ben, and shook her head.

Soon all the unloaded trucks were driven away. The door to the garage was closed, and all the people who had come out of it were gone. The only thing out of place was the man lying on the ground and the three people crouched beside him.

"My mother needs to know," Patrice said, wiping her eyes. "If it's possible, she'll want his body."

"How far can you fly?" Dion asked Ben.

"Far," Ben said.

"Shank and Patrice are from a farm about sixty miles away. Do you think you can take them there before the sun comes up?"

"No problem," Ben said.

"Good," Dion replied. "Patrice will go with you and make sure you find your way back to the city."

16. The Gift of Gills

It was midmorning, and Ben was still not back. Breakfast was over, and everyone was busy with their assigned tasks. Off and on, Charla worried about Ben but spent most of her time thinking about the special mission she was going on. She could hardly wait. It was her first time off-world with the Watcher's blessing. She felt lucky to still be a Chosen of the Guardian after getting caught sneaking through the portal to visit Earth. Her immediate goal was to be so brilliant on this, her first real mission, that she would completely erase her past mistakes and be guaranteed many more future trips off-world. Everyone would agree she'd been essential in getting this mission off to a good start by rescuing the prisoners. She had reminded several people that they would still be locked up without her help. Perhaps that's why the Resistance leader chose her for this mission.

She didn't believe it was just the fact that she could stay underwater for a very long time, thanks to the gills behind her ears.

Charla had a loose skirt made of lightweight material, which would make it easier to transform back and forth between human legs and a Mer tail. On her head was the wig she'd put on before she stepped through the portal to come to Mellish. Her closely cropped greenish-blond hair would only pass as normal on her own world as well as on Earth, where people dyed their hair all kinds of colors.

Contact lenses, specially created to make a mermaid's eyes appear human, covered her eyes. They hid the fact there was no white surrounding a darker pupil.

She was pacing back and forth even though it was unwise to use up energy by staying in human form. She should have been sitting quietly somewhere in her natural form. But she was never very good at sitting still. So, she walked back and forth as she waited. Finally, Mara arrived in the company of an older woman dressed in shabby clothes.

"Are you ready?" Mara asked.

"Of course." I've been ready for years, but no one's given me a chance to prove myself until now.

"This is Paulie. She will be your grandmother for this mission," Mara said.

Charla said hello to Paulie, using her most respectful tone, the one she reserved for Watchers and for people who were significantly older than she was.

"Remember, your job is to locate the Medallion, not retrieve it. We want you to bring back information so we can come up with a good plan."

"Why don't I just find the Medallion and bring it back with me now?" Charla asked.

"I don't want you to do that," Mara said. "We get one chance, and we need to take our best shot. If we mess things up, it will be a long time before we get another opportunity."

In Charla's opinion, people spent far too much time looking for the perfect plan when they could just get the job done with a whole lot less trouble. "Yes, but I don't see why you wouldn't want me to grab the Medallion and bring it back with me now," she said.

"Believe me; the Medallion won't be in a place where it can easily be grabbed."

"What if he takes it off and puts it beside the bed when he sleeps?"

"We have it from a reliable source that he does not keep the Medallion with him."

"Still, a single person can do what a whole crowd can't."

Mara frowned. "You've heard my instructions. Do you think you can carry them out?"

Charla wasn't happy, but she gave a brief nod. She would comply with her instructions. She didn't want a bad report getting back to the Lushakan Watcher. "So, when are we leaving?" she asked.

"Right away," Mara responded. "But first of all, you need to replace the contact lenses in your eyes with these."

"What's wrong with the ones I'm wearing."

"Nothing, but these are in Grek's database and have no black marks against them. Drones can safely scan these contact lenses. Please don't lose them as we have very few like these. They require hiding the death of someone who has never been in trouble."

Charla took the contact lenses out of their small box and put them in her eyes.

Paulie and Charla caught a people mover that would take them within four blocks of the palace. As they traveled, Paulie filled her in on their cover story. They were from a small town named Apea, an hour away from the city by train. Paulie was dying and had gotten special permission to come into Nortown because she wanted to show her granddaughter the palace where she'd worked when she was her age.

"Hopefully, this story will get us close enough to sit beside the fountain outside the palace," Paulie said. "As you've been told, it connects to one inside. The water circulates between the two of them. When it is safe to do so, you will slide into the pool and find a place to hide until the water changes direction and begins to flow into the palace. For the next few days, there will be a street cleaner in the plaza wearing a yellow hat with the words 'life is better with luka beans. 'That cleaner will be one of us and will help you get back to the Resistance."

When they got off the people mover, Grek's image appeared on the side of a nearby building. Paulie and Charla stood and watched him for a moment.

"People of Mellish," Grek said. "It is my great privilege to lead you through these troubling times. I do not know why previous generations did not realize the wisdom of having the Watcher also be the president. I bring so much more experience and wisdom to this position than anyone else alive could do. With me as your leader, you are on the road to prosperity."

"A good number of my neighbors believe what Grek says is true," Paulie said. "They argue that he doesn't make mistakes like an ordinary person would. They say the restrictions of our freedoms is just temporary. When I ask them where their prosperity is, they say Grek can't fix every problem at once, and it makes sense to them that things will worsen before they get better. They blame all the trouble on those who resist his authority. Nothing I say convinces them otherwise. A friend of mine, who is more outspoken than I am, disappeared. I worry about Mila all the time."

With those words, Paulie took Charla by the arm, and they walked toward the palace. They were three blocks away when Charla noticed the increased security. There were more drones in one place than she'd ever seen before.

There were soldiers with weapons standing on every street corner. Charla could feel their eyes watching them as they walked toward the palace. Drones were constantly swooping down to get a closer look. More than one scanned their eyes, and Charla had to stop herself from batting them out of the air. When they got to the plaza, two soldiers intercepted them and asked what they were doing. Paulie gave them her prepared story about working in the palace when a previous President lived there. She told them how she used to come out on her breaks and sit beside the fountain watching people come and go. Paulie spoke of wanting to relive her memories with her granddaughter before she died. Paulie added that the doctors had told her she had three months to live.

The soldiers stared at them for a few seconds. Then one of them took the large bag Paulie carried and carefully searched through it. Charla's bag was tied to her leg underneath her full skirt. If the soldier decided to pat her down, he might find it. She held her breath, afraid he might decide to do just that.

"Fine, you can sit near the fountain for a few minutes, but don't stay too long," the older of the two soldiers said.

They reached their destination and chose a spot where they would be partially hidden by the fountain when it was flowing. There were two soldiers standing at the palace door who would have a clear view of them. There were also guards standing at each corner of the palace and throughout the plaza. Charla took off her sweater and slipped her feet out of her shoes. Paulie picked them up and put them in her bag. Charla had a light pair of shoes inside the waterproof bag hidden underneath her skirt.

"You have to wait," Paulie reminded her. "Until this fountain stops flowing. You've got three minutes before the water flow changes direction again. Don't leave the pipe at the other end until the water stops moving to avoid being sucked into the pump inside the palace."

Charla and Paulie waited for the guards at the door and on the plaza to look away at the same time. Then, Charla pushed herself backward, shrinking, and transforming as she fell. As soon as she was in the water, Charla tied her skirt up so it wouldn't get in the way of her tailfin. The stale water tasted like dead fish left in the sun too long, so she kept her head out of the water and continued to breathe as a human. She was floating on the surface when she heard a guard come and speak with Paulie.

"What happened to your granddaughter?" the guard asked. "She was here just a moment ago."

"She said she had to go meet some friends. Guess she wasn't all that interested in her grannie's stories."

"But, I would have seen her go."

"She moves pretty fast when she wants to."

"Huh," the guard snorted in a way that expressed his skepticism.

Charla ducked under a leaf floating on the surface just before the guard stepped close to the pond and looked into the water. "I think you'd better leave before I arrest you," she heard the guard say. "We don't appreciate tricksters this close to the palace."

A few seconds later, the pump stopped working, and the fountain stopped flowing. It was a sign that the one inside had turned on. It was time for Charla to enter the pipe and go with the flow of water into the palace.

The water was putrid. She hated the taste of it. She could tell that the same water had been circling through the pipes for a very long time. Her gills started quivering soon after she switched to breathing through them. She dived down to where the water left through a drain. There was a mesh grate over it with holes big enough for a housefly to go through. Part of it was covered by paper and debris that the wind had carried in, but she was able to push it aside and enter the pipe. As soon as she was through the mesh, she grew as large as she could and still travel inside the pipe. It was pitch black, and she couldn't see anything, not even with her mermaid eyes, which could see in the dark depths of ocean caves. Since she couldn't see anything, she closed her eyes to protect them from the putrid water. She slit them open every few seconds to make sure she wasn't near the end of the pipe.

Charla knew she was getting close when she saw the light, but she couldn't tell if there was a wire mesh because of the glare. She was almost on it when the lines of wire revealed themselves. Relieved, Charla grabbed hold of one of the wires with both hands and stretched her body out across several other lines. She was large enough that the water current could not carry her through the mesh. Meanwhile, she had started to feel faint. It was either her body's reaction to the polluted water, or there wasn't enough oxygen in it for her gills to capture. They were quivering as she attempted to bring in the oxygen she needed.

Charla kept pushing back against the darkness that threatened to engulf her as she waited for it to be safe to leave the pipe. She was so caught up in the struggle to stay conscious that she almost missed it when the pump shut off. Charla had gripped the wire so tight it left marks on her hands when she let go. She shrunk in size, pushed her way through the mesh, and swam quickly away from the pump. She swam with her eyes closed and her hands stretched out in front of her. When she touched the side of the pond, she swam up the wall. When her face cleared the surface, she gulped a lungful of fresh air through her mouth and opened her eyes. She floated on her back and breathed deeply until her strength returned. It was time to address the next challenge. How was she going to get out of the pond without being seen?

Charla decided it was best to stay in the pond until later on in the night when fewer people would be around. Hearing footsteps, she found a place where some of the brick had broken away, forming a small cave. Charla climbed in, leaned her back against the wall, and waited with her tail fin hanging down into the water. Like all Mer, who could transform into a human, she needed time in her true form while in contact with water to stay healthy. Even this brackish water was better than no water at all as long as she didn't have to use her gills for breathing. After a while, she closed her eyes and surprised herself by falling asleep. When she woke up, the lights had been turned down low, and it was quiet.

Charla transformed her tail into legs and grew until she could stand on the bottom of the pool and peek over the side. She was in the rotunda of a four-story building. Above her was the large glass dome that was central to the palace. Moonlight was shining through it. Mellish had two moons, the second one was larger and brighter than the first and rose after midnight. The amount of light suggested the second moon had recently risen.

A sweeping staircase led up to a second level; then a smaller one continued to the third and fourth levels of the palace. The front door wall was the only one without balconies. There was a balcony on each floor except the ground floor she was on. When she looked up, she noticed guards standing near the staircase on each floor above her. The ground floor of the foyer appeared empty, so she crouched down as she grew enough to be able to throw her body over the rock wall. She sprang up and over to land on the floor of the foyer in a place hidden from those standing guard above her.

"Hey, did you see that?" a voice above her called out.

"I didn't see anything," a second voice said.

"What did you see?" a third voice asked.

"I thought I saw someone come out of the pond, but then whoever it was, just disappeared," the first voice said.

"There's nothing there now, but we'll have Hank check it out when he returns the second voice said.

Charla took off her skirt and wrung it dry before stowing it in her bag. Under her skirt, she had been wearing leggings which she left on. Charla put the shoes she'd carried in her bag on her feet. Looking up, she noticed several intersecting lines shining in the air. She quickly realized they were part of the security system. It had been pure luck that had caused her to jump out in a spot that was between two intersecting light beams. Some were close to the ground so that a full-grown person could not crawl underneath. Others hung high in the air.

Charla made herself short enough to walk underneath the lines of light so she wouldn't trigger any alarms. Staying close to the pond wall, she walked away from the outside door toward the staircase. Four arches were leading from the rotunda into hallways. She saw light shining through a partially opened door down the hallway on the left side of the staircase. Charla decided it was an excellent place to begin her search. Her choice was confirmed as the right one when she caught the sweet aroma of bread baking. When she stepped through the open door, she discovered an industrial-sized kitchen. She hid behind a broom that stood nearby. An oven door was open, and a portly man with dark hair peppered with grey was just taking one of the racks out. On it were several pans of freshly baked bread. He placed the rack on a counter beside some newly baked pie. The smells and sights made Charla realize how hungry she was.

17. The Watcher of Mellish

These night shifts just kill me," said a voice off to the right. Charla jumped. She hadn't realized someone was sitting a couple of feet away. A young woman sat on a chair with a cup in her hand. She was only a couple of years older than Charla. Her red hair was braided and tied into a loop on either side of her head. Freckles dotted her cheeks, and there was a significant number on her nose.

"Do a good job, and you'll be able to join the day shift. I wish I could, but as the palace baker, I'm stuck on nights."

The baker rubbed his hands on his dirty apron. "Although, you might wish you were back on nights. It can get busy during the day when the Generals are here."

"I'd prefer being busy rather than just sitting here waiting for the bell to ring."

"I'll get his Excellency's tray ready just in case he wakes up early." The baker walked into a cold storage area and came out with a glass pan covered with a lid. When he took off the cover, Charla caught the faint aroma of freshly caught fish. The baker took two fish and laid them on a chopping block. He then filleted one of them by cutting the flesh off the bones and removing the skin. He then cut off the head and tail and chopped what remained into smaller pieces. He pushed the tail off the counter, and it dropped to the floor. Charla ran under the counter toward it to see if there was still some meat left. She had just about reached it when a cat-like looking creature pounced on the fishtail and carried it away. Charla was looking for a place to hide when a second tail landed on the floor. She got her knife out and sliced some flesh off. She popped it in her mouth and was cutting a second piece when the cat batted her aside. It picked up the second fishtail and growled at Charla as it ate.

Charla had tumbled into a table leg, and her breath was knocked out of her. She lay still for a moment and then pushed herself up off the ground. The cat finished its second fishtail and was doing a creepy crawl toward Charla with its nose and whiskers twitching. It seemed unsure of what she was. Charla worried that the cat might be wondering how she would taste. She desperately searched for a place to hide where the cat couldn't reach her. There was a crack where two cupboards joined in a corner. Charla backed up toward it, keeping her eyes on the cat. It followed her. When it increased its speed, she turned and ran, but too late.

The cat caught her and flipped her in the air. When she came down, she was looking up at the cat, which was holding her loosely in its claws. She could feel its whiskers and smell its fishy breath on her neck. Her left arm was immobile, but the right was free and held her knife. The cat pulled her towards itself and opened its mouth. Charla had no choice. She grew to be the size of a rat and slashed the cat's nose with her knife. It yowled and let her go. She slowly shrank in size as she ran toward the crack in the cupboard. She was the size of a housefly when she reached it. Once safely inside the gap, she turned around to discover the cat looking in. There was a line of blood on its nose. It was making a weird growling sound as it sat there with its tail twitching. Charla shuddered to think of what would have happened if it had caught her.

"It sounds like the cat's found something," the girl said.

"I'm not sure what it could be," the baker said. "It's too small for a mouse. Besides, the cat's doing a great job keeping the kitchen free of them. I'm glad my cousin suggested one. But now it's time for it to go out. The day shift won't want it underfoot." He scooped up the cat and carried it away.

Charla ran out from where she was hiding. It seemed important to see how the baker would put the cat outside. He opened a small door on the far wall of the kitchen. It opened into what looked like a secret garden. There was a bench not far from the door with a hedge behind it. Charla wondered what kind of guard was kept on the back door and where it was in relation to the rest of the palace.

Not long after that, a bell rang. The baker quickly cut a couple of pieces of warm bread and placed them on a tray with the fish. He also put a jug of water with a glass on the tray. "There you go, Selina," the baker said.

The girl stood, picked up the tray, and left through the door. Charla followed her. She had to run as fast as she could to match the girl's walking pace and knew she couldn't keep this up for long. It turned out she didn't need to. Selina stopped and pushed a button. Charla heard the sound of mechanical movement and assumed an elevator was on its way to the floor they were on. One of Selina's shoelaces was near the ground. Charla jumped up and grabbed hold of it, then crawled up on top of the shoe. When the door opened, Charla rode Selina's foot into the elevator. It didn't go up as she expected, but down.

The elevator stopped and the door opened. A soldier stood guard, his weapon was out, and pointed at the elevator. He put it away when he saw that it was a girl carrying a food tray.

"Hey, Selina," he said.

"Hey, yourself," Selina replied.

Charla held on tight as Selina stepped out of the elevator. To the left, there was a long hallway to a heavy metal door. The door was closed, and a soldier was standing guard outside it. Selina turned to the right and walked toward a soldier standing guard outside another closed door. The soldier knocked on the door, and when a voice said to enter, he opened it.

Close to the door on the left was a table with seating for more than twenty people. Beyond the conference table was a stone fireplace sitting between two large windows that went from the middle of the wall to the ceiling. There were three large overstuffed couches and four chairs sitting in a semi-circle in front of the large fireplace.

When Charla looked out the window, she saw a courtyard surrounded by a high concrete wall. Over the wall, she could see the tops of trees. It was early in the morning. The sun was just rising, and the sky had a pink glow. Charla realized that the palace must have been constructed on a hill to make this room ground level. The kitchen, one floor up, was also ground level.

Three doors were leading off from this room. Selina headed to the first open door on the right side. Charla found herself in a large office with walls covered in bookshelves. On the left side, near the door, was a table that had an inbox and an outbox for mail. A large monitor hung on the wall to the right of the door. On the monitor was a message Charla had seen when they walked to the palace. The sound was muted. The desk was L shaped. Grek was sitting on the long side, facing the monitor, writing a letter. Piles of paper were stacked on the short wing of the desk.

Charla caught a glimpse of Grek before the desk got in her way. He was an older man, whose thin white hair seemed to have a green tinge to it. He was wearing a bathrobe. Charla slid down the shoelace and hid behind the leg of the small table that stood near the door.

"Good morning, your Excellency," Selina said. "Where would you like your tray?"

What kind of Watcher would trade his work on behalf of the Guardian for the privilege of being called your Excellency? Charla wondered. What world had he come from? She hadn't asked that question before. She had assumed he was from Mellish, but Watchers did not always come from the world they were born into. In fact, when she thought about it, they were more often from a different world than their own. The exception was her world of Lushaka.

'There is nothing good about this morning," Grek growled as he crumpled the paper he was holding in his hand. "The Resistance broke into five storage facilities last night. They succeeded in carrying away food from every single one of them. Food that should be eaten by citizens who are loyal to me. I knew those escaped prisoners were going to be trouble."

Charla saw a fleeting smile cross Selina's face before she could replace it with a blank stare. It turned into a frown when Grek kept speaking. "We'll see how much support the Resistance still has when there are reduced rations because of them." Then he added, "No mercy next time. I'll kill them all."

"Reduced rations will be very difficult for people. Some don't feel the rations are enough as it is."

"They're just greedy," Grek snarled. "They've never had it so good."

"Will that be all your Excellency?" Selina asked. Her voice was quivering.

"Yes," Grek said. "Leave me."

"Yes, your Excellency, I'll be back later for your tray," Selina walked out of the office. Charla stayed where she was. She could just see Grek's head over the desk. She couldn't see what was under the desk without moving to a different location.

Grek lifted his head, turned toward the door, and watched Selina walk away. Charla gasped. It wasn't his eyes that gave him away. He was wearing contacts just like she was. But she caught a glimpse of gills behind his ears. He kept his hair long to hide them, but by turning his head back and forth, he'd given them away. A human seeing them would just think it was an odd scar, but Charla recognized it for what it was.

Grek picked up a piece of the raw fish and bit into it. Another giveaway for anyone who knew fish was a Mers preferred diet. Charla moved from the table she was hiding behind to where Grek was sitting to see under the desk and confirm her suspicion. Just as she suspected, there were no human legs, but a Mer tail was sitting on a footstool. A human coming into the office would not be able to see it without bending down.

Charla closed her eyes and leaned against a chair leg. She felt a deep sense of shame. It had never crossed her mind that one of her people would be capable of this kind of treason. She had always thought her people were above deception and would never betray the trust of the Guardian. Humans, yes. Dragonborn, certainly, but not Mer. It made her even more determined to stop Grek. He could not be allowed to continue dishonoring her people. She moved back to her original hiding place and waited to see what he would do next. A half-hour later, he transformed his tail into legs and walked across the room with the fireplace to a door on the left hand. Charla followed him into a short corridor. To move faster, she grew to be the size of a mouse, hoping he wouldn't turn and look behind him. He walked down the corridor and opened a door. The door was closing when Charla dove through it. The floor was wet, and she slid across it to stop at the edge of the pool. She considered dropping into the water and spending some time in her mermaid form but knew it might be hard for her to get out of the pool without growing larger. Instead, she moved as close to the door as she could while still being able to see what Grek was doing. She was lucky he was preoccupied and hadn't seen her.

As she watched, he took off his robe and lay it on a deck chair, and waded naked into the water. Charla closed her eyes for a moment. She had no interest in seeing his bare butt. When she opened them again, he was waist-high in the water, and that's when she noticed he had something around his neck. Was it the Medallion? Was the information the Resistance had wrong? Did he keep it around his neck at all times?

Grek transformed his legs into a tail and dove headfirst into the water. He swam toward the middle of the pool, where there was a glass structure. There was something inside the structure, but Charla couldn't quite see what it was. He swam around the outside of the structure several times on the surface, then dove down and swam around it under the water. Charla crept closer to the pool to get a closer look. Something was not quite right. Then she realized what it was. Grek had entered an underwater glass tunnel that circled the center. A few minutes later, Charla saw his distorted image in a glass room that was above water. He transformed his tail into legs and stood up inside it. When he picked up what hung around his neck, Charla realized it was not the Medallion but a key. Grek used it to open the door of a metal box at the center of the glass room. He pulled something out and put it around his neck. From what she understood, he only had to touch the Medallion once a day to be able to enjoy the long life it gave to those who held it. If he wanted to be in communion with the Guardian and have a mystical connection with Mellish, he needed to wear the Medallion all the time. He might still wish he still had full use of the Guardian's gifts, but he couldn't keep them without on-going communication with the Guardian, which he didn't want. He was simply using the Medallion to extend his already very long life.

Charla left the swimming pool and ran back through the short corridor. She now knew where Grek kept the Medallion; all she had to do now was figure out how to retrieve it. Charla ran to Grek's office and once there grew to full height. She rummaged through the papers on the desk. Near the top, she found a report from the jailer who watched the prisoners from other worlds. As she read, it became clear that these prisoners were in the same prison she'd helped the others escape from. If she'd only known, she would have tried to free them at the same time. The jailer was pleased to let Grek know that Truehaven was still working well as a prison for their special prisoners despite the escape. Repairs on those parts of the prison damaged by the fire were finished, and the cells were available for anyone Grek wanted to send. The mind-altering work with the Chosen had just begun, and he was sure they would eventually agree to support his Excellency. In fact, by the time he finished with them, they would be more than willing to join Grek in his battle for liberation from the tyranny imposed by the Guardian. If that failed, then per Grek's instructions, they would be killed.

She was about to shrink back down and hide when she noticed some papers sitting on the inbox shelf near the door. She took them out and looked through them. One caused her heart to skip a beat. It was from the warden of a different jail who reported that a Resistance member died under torture, but that he may have disclosed the location of the Resistance before doing so. He said they were living in tunnels underneath the city. The prisoner had given him the location of one of the entrances. He planned to check it out and let Grek know what he found. They were keeping the dead man's head on ice, so they could use his eyes to gain entrance into the tunnel later in the day.

Charla was horrified. The brave people who were resisting oppression were in grave danger. She wondered if Grek had seen this message. Should she remove it or leave it where it was? Finally, she folded it up and put it in her pocket. She was still shrinking when Grek walked through the door. Fortunately, she was hidden by the table, and he didn't see her. She thought about what she'd read. It would not be easy if the Resistance had to move. It would make it harder to rescue the Chosen and do what they needed to do to stop Grek.

She needed to get back as soon as she could to warn them, but she also needed to do something about the key. Without it, she would never be able to get to the Medallion. She couldn't steal the original. If she did, Grek would know, and he would simply change the lock. Of course, she could grab the key and get the Medallion tonight while he was asleep. But what if she was caught? The information she had was too important to risk. Besides, she had to follow orders. The Watcher on her world and the one on Earth already had questions about her suitability. She needed others to see her as someone who was able to follow orders. It was almost more important than being successful, at least for her, if not for the people of Mellish. What she needed was a way to make a copy of the key. Wax would work. Where was she to get wax? Did it even exist in this world? If they didn't have wax, they might have something else that could work. How could she find what she needed?

She now knew why she'd been selected to come to Mellish. No one other than a Mer could enter the swimming pool and go through the underwater tube to the place where Grek kept the Medallion. A Human could never hold their breath long enough. She was certain a Dragonborn couldn't either. The tube allowed for a body to swim through, but not a body with an oxygen tank attached to it if such a thing even existed in this world. The only world she'd heard tell of such things was Earth. Only a Mer could get the Medallion. If they had a copy of the key, they might have some chance of retrieving it.

The Resistance leaders wanted her to find a way into the palace that did not involve shrinking and going through a pipe filled with water. The only thing she could think of was the kitchen door the cook put the cat out of. How did you get to that door from the outside? Was it well guarded? Did the kitchen staff go through that door when their shift changed? It would be helpful to be able to ask one of them this question.

Thinking of the kitchen staff brought Selina to mind. She remembered the slight smile appearing on her face when she heard that the Resistance had attacked the warehouses. Charla thought about that smile. She thought about how helpful it would be to have someone inside the palace to assist them. But it was very risky, and Charla doubted the Resistance leader would approve of her making a plan of her own, but Mara was not here. She hadn't seen the smile herself, and Charla doubted she could convince her that it meant Selina was on their side. Charla wondered if she could find a way to be alone with Selina and learn more about her. Finding someone to help her might be the only way of getting her hands on the Medallion.

Grek walked out of the door. As soon as he was gone, Charla grew in size and ran over to the desk. She sat on it and immediately shrunk in size. Then she stood and jumped onto the tray that had contained the bread and fish. She was standing on it when there was a knock on the outside door. Grek said to come in and the door opened.

"Your Excellency, I'm back to pick up your tray," she heard Selina say.

"Were you back earlier?" Grek asked.

"No, I wasn't," Selina said.

"There's no point in lying. The soldiers outside the door will tell me if you came in a few minutes ago."

"They will tell you I didn't," Selina said. "Why are you asking me this question?"

"I'm certain someone has been in my office, and you are the only person authorized to come in at this time of day."

How did he know? Charla wondered. *Did I leave something out of place, or does Grek have enough of the*

Guardian's gift still at work in him to know something without depending on the evidence that his senses provide?

"Excellency, please ask the soldiers at the door. They will tell you it wasn't me."

"If it wasn't you, who was it?"

"I don't know." Selina's voice was shaking. "Shall I take your tray now?"

"Yes, go ahead."

Charla heard footsteps walking toward the office and moved under the plate's rim, pulling the dirty napkin over her. Selina picked up the tray and carried it and Charla toward the door. As they exited, Charla heard Grek mutter, "Maybe it's time for a change of guard."

18. Back to the City

Ben and Patrice had just finished breakfast when a neighbor arrived. After being introduced to Ben and offering his condolences to Shank's mother, Portia, Chet shared information from the city. The warehouses' attack had become known even though the government tried to suppress information about successful Resistance attacks. A witness claimed to see a dragon flying out of the city not long afterward. There was an increase in the number of drones flying around the city's outskirts, and Chet assumed they were looking for a dragon. "How stupid is that," he concluded. "There is no such thing as dragons."

"Speaking of the Resistance," Portia said. "I understand you have some connection with them."

"Where did you hear that?"

"My son Shank told me you helped him once in a while. I know he was part of the Resistance."

"He shouldn't have told you that. It's not something I want the world to know."

"Ben is part of the Resistance, and he needs to get back into the city. Would you be willing to help him?"

Chet stared at Ben for a moment. "Were you the one who brought Shank's body home to his mother?"

"Yes," Ben replied.

"That was good of you. How did you manage without getting caught?" Chet asked. "Never mind. It's better that I don't know."

"Can you help?" Portia asked again.

"I'm scheduled to take a truckload of shaffs into the city later today. Some of it is earmarked for the Resistance. Ben can hide in a sack."

"What are shaffs?" Ben asked.

"Everyone knows what shaffs are," Chet said.

"Ben took a fall on his head," Patrice patted Ben's arm.

"Remember, Ben honey, we had shaffs for supper last night," Portia said. "It was the yellow vegetable."

Patrice turned toward her mother. "I want to go back to the city with him. Is there room for two of us to be hidden in the back of your truck?" she asked Chet

"Are you sure you'll be okay to travel, with the knock on your head?" Chet asked Ben.

"I'll be fine," Ben said. "My memory is better today than it was yesterday."

"Please stay here," Portia said to her daughter. "I don't want to lose another child in this fight."

"If I don't resist, I'll lose myself," Patrice said. "I can't live in a world where there is no freedom and no justice—a world where there is one rule for the rich and another for the rest of us. I can't live in a world where people cannot express what is in their hearts. My spirit will die, and I will waste away in such a world. Please, let me go so I can fight. That is my only hope of continuing to really live."

Tears slipped down Portia's face as she turned to her neighbor. "Do you have room for my daughter, Chet?"

"I can make room," he said. "If we can get them into the city, they should be safe. With so many drones flying around the outskirts, Grek will have fewer eyes on the city itself."

Ben didn't like this plan. He'd been looking forward to another flight as a dragon, but he could see the wisdom of going back another way. They would be watching for a dragon, not people hidden in sacks of vegetables.

By mid-afternoon, they were bouncing along in the back of a truck. Ben and Patrice were hidden in large sacks containing the shaffs, which resembled carrots in Ben's mind. They were larger than the average carrot and more yellow than orange, but they were the same shape. Chet placed them near the back of the truck with more sacks piled in and around them. One was partly resting on top of Ben's legs. Another was partially on top of his body. It made it so he couldn't move at all. They hadn't traveled very far before his feet started to tingle and then became painful.

Chet had warned him not to move the sacks off of his body. He'd stressed that they needed to cover him as much as possible, so he fought against the desire to push them away. Ben had a growing desire to break out of the sack, leave the truck, and soar into the air in his dragon form. He knew it would be a huge mistake to do so, but the desire to transform was overwhelming. A couple of times, he felt himself begin the transformation, and he had to fight to stop himself. He guessed this was another symptom of the Wrathborn season Miss Templeton had warned him about.

She told him he would find himself being unreasonable and have less control over his reactions. She had said he needed to be careful not to make extreme responses that didn't fit the situation. As far as he was concerned, it hadn't been a huge problem yet. He didn't think his reactions had been that extreme. Although Miss Templeton had warned him that he would not always be a good judge of how appropriate his behavior was when caught in the season of Wrathborn.

Ben didn't know how much time had passed when the truck stopped. Chet had said Grek's security forces would likely have a roadblock and do a search of the truck. He had been warned not to move or say a word when the truck stopped without Chet's permission. He could feel the fire burning in his belly. The dragon part of him wanted nothing more than to burn those soldiers to a crisp. The human part of him was appalled. He fought to push down the fire and keep it from growing too hot to contain.

"Show me your papers," a voice said, followed by silence. "What do you have in the truck?"

"I have shaffs for the city," Chet said. "I like to think they will end up on the table of Grek himself, and the great leader will wonder who grows such a delicious crop. I dream of an exclusive contract to provide them for the palace."

"Right," the soldier said in a voice that sounded bored. "Open the back."

Ben's face was close to the opening of the bag to make it easier for him to breathe. He could peek through it with his right eye. He watched as the back of the truck opened. Two soldiers stood on either side of Chet. The one on the right roughly pushed the farmer aside. He cut the tie on the nearest sack open and Shaffs spilled out. The other guard held what looked like an extra-long walking stick with a thin metal tip on the end. He started sticking it into the other sacks. He began with the ones closest to him and then moved toward the back of the truck where Ben and Patrice were hiding. Ben now knew why Chet insisted they have sacks over their lower body and legs. Ben wished he'd known why. He would have done a better job of making sure he was protected.

He held his breath as the point of the stick came toward his sack. He was afraid there were not enough shaffs on top of him to keep from being poked: Afraid he would call out in pain if he was. He bit his lip as he felt the point pressing in. It sunk deep into one of the shaffs and quickly pulled out without reaching him. The guard had to stretch to reach where he lay and was not able to press the point in as far as he had with the ones closest to the tailgate. Ben guessed that was why Chet had put him and Patrice close to the cab of the truck.

A few seconds later, the door closed, and the truck started up. Less than a half-hour passed before the truck stopped again. When the back door opened, Ben saw the inside of a building.

"Are you both okay?" Chet asked.

"I'm fine, except for my legs," Ben said. "I can't believe how painful not being able to move can be."

"I'm…not…okay," Patrice said in a halting voice.

"What's wrong?" Ben asked, worried. Patrice did not reply, but Ben could hear the jagged sound of her breathing. He hadn't heard it before because of the sounds from the truck as it drove down the road.

Chet jumped into the truck and scrambled over the sacks to get to Patrice. He pulled the shaffs off her chest and saw no sign that anything was wrong. He pulled a sack off her legs, and that's when he saw the blood. He pulled her toward the open door as gently as he could and helped her out of the sack. When she was free, he laid her on a pallet. The spear had gone through her thigh.

"Hey, can I get some help?" Chet heard Ben say. He ignored the boy as he tried to figure out what to do about Patrice's leg. He couldn't imagine going back and telling his friend and neighbor that her daughter was dead.

"Hey, I'm stuck in this sack," he heard Ben say. "I'm having a hard time getting out on my own."

"I'll be there in a bit," Chet said. "Patrice has been injured." He went and searched for the cleanest rag he could find and tied it around the top of the girl's leg to try to stop the flow of blood. Then he went and pushed a buzzer on the wall before climbing into the truck to help Ben.

Ben couldn't get himself out because the sack was tied with a complicated knot. He couldn't get his hand out far enough to untie it. It was a relief when Chet climbed into the truck and untied the knot for him. He removed the two bags covering Ben's body but left him lying in the truck still in the sack as he hurried back to look after Patrice. It wasn't as easy to get out as Ben thought it would be. The sacks on top of him were gone, but shaffs still pushed in on him from both sides. He pushed his arms up past his head and through the narrow opening to enlarge it and then forced the sack downward until he could sit up. Then he pushed the bag down over his legs and used his elbows to crawl over the sacks to the open door. A complaint about an absence of needed help rose to his lips but not spoken when he looked over and saw Patrice lying on the pallet, her face pale, and her pant leg soaked with blood. He slid off the truck and onto his feet to go to her, but his legs gave way. They had gone to sleep and wouldn't hold him. He grabbed the tailgate and pulled himself up. Pain shot up his legs. "Are you all right?" he asked Patrice as soon as he was able.

"Don't worry," she whispered. "It's not as back as it looks."

"You did well not to cry out when they speared you," Ben said. "I'm not sure I could have done the same."

"Of course you could have," Patrice said.

"I'm sorry, I thought I put enough shaffs overtop your legs," Chet said.

"It's not your fault," Patrice said.

"I hope your mother sees it that way."

"Please don't tell her," Patrice said.

Chet took three sacks of shaffs out of the truck and laid them near where Patrice lay. "Will you be okay until the Resistance arrives?" he asked. "They should be here soon."

"I'll be fine," Patrice said.

"Good. I should be on my way. There will be questions I don't want to answer if I fail to arrive at the scheduled time."

"I'll be okay," Patrice assured him again.

"Wait, you can't leave her here bleeding," Ben said.

"Yes, he can. Chet needs to go, so he doesn't bring suspicion on himself," Patrice said.

Chet moved Ben aside and pulled out another sack of shaffs. He then reorganized the load to make it look like everything that should be there was. "I'm sorry to leave you, but I do need to get to my destination on time."

Chet went to a monitor hanging on the wall near the door. He poked some buttons, and different images came up on the screen. When he satisfied himself that it was safe, he opened the warehouse door and drove his truck out. The door closed immediately afterward, leaving Patrice and Ben inside.

"Chet is one of those heroes who does what he can to keep the Resistance fed," Patrice said. "I didn't know that before. I'm glad I do now. I'll never eat another shaff without being thankful that one of my neighbors is risking his life to provide it."

A few minutes later, a wooden panel on the side of the warehouse swung open. There was a shelving unit attached to the wall, which swung out with it. It was the last place Ben would have looked for a concealed entry. Kudos to whoever had designed it. Four men walked through, each one wearing a helmet with a light attached to it.

"What have we here?" a muscular man with red hair asked.

Patrice sat up and explained the events that had brought them to the warehouse. When she finished, she reached out her hand so the red-haired man could help her stand. As soon as she did, her legs gave way. "Just give me a moment," Patrice said. "I'll be fine. The wound isn't that bad."

"You're not fine," the man said. "Walking on that leg is going to make the bleeding worse."

The red-haired man picked up a sack and pressed it into Ben's arms. "You carry this, and I'll carry Patrice." The bag was heavy, and the weight made Ben's feet and legs feel like there was a horde of bees stinging him. The red-haired man picked up Patrice and led the way to the open panel in the wall. The remaining three men picked up shaffs and followed him. Ben stumbled along behind them.

"Wait," one of the men said as Ben stepped through the panel opening. He laid his sack down and took a helmet from a peg on the wall, turned on the light, and pressed it onto Ben's head. He then closed the panel leading into the garage and picked up his sack. "Follow me," he said.

19. Wrathborn Season

When they arrived back at the headquarters, Ben heard singing. He dropped off the bag of shaffs and headed toward the dining hall. Jared was standing just inside the doorway when he got there.

"Hi Jared," Ben said. "Glad to see you made it as a Chosen on Lushaka."

"Thanks to you and Charla. I'm grateful every time I think about how you saved my brother from being eaten by a rogue dragon. And of course, I'm grateful for the part you played in helping me become a Chosen. In case you wonder, Charla's been amazing. She vouched for me every time a Mer said a human didn't belong."

"She's a good person to have in your corner even though she can be annoying at times."

"That's for sure," Jared agreed.

"Where is she, by the way?" Ben asked.

"She's been sent out on a special assignment." Jared paused, and when he spoke again, he said every word slowly and distinctly. "On...her...own."

Ben and Jared gave each other a look that conveyed without words their agreement that it was a bad idea to let Charla go on her own.

"The song they're singing reminds me of one we sing on Earth; 'for he's a jolly good fellow.'" Ben said. "What's going on?"

"They're honoring the teams that went out and brought back food. They're choosing one person from each team for special recognition. Meet the king of oil." Jared pulled out a handmade cardboard crown and stuck it on his head. "It's all just for fun. You should go in; your team will be next. Who knows, they might crown you King of Luka Beans."

When Ben entered the dining hall, people were sitting at tables. He searched for and found Allison, who was sitting next to Trevor. Someone Ben didn't recognize was holding up a cardboard crown. "Next, we're going to recognize the King of Luka Beans. We now have enough to last for months." There was a groan mixed with cheers at those words. "We have tried and failed to get beans from that warehouse before, but we didn't have Trevor with us then. Trevor is the King of Luka Beans."

Allison leaned into Trevor and kissed him.

Ben couldn't help himself. Fire exploded from deep within. He turned away as quickly as he could so he wouldn't hurt the people around him. He tried to force the flame down as he ran out of the dining hall. He went to the storeroom where he'd left the shaffs, and once there, he let the dragonfire flare bright and hot.

Ben felt justified in his anger. All Trevor had done was make a hole in a wall and drive a truck through it. He hadn't taken the risks Ben and the others had. He hadn't been under constant weapons 'fire. Shank, Jake, Florrie, Patrice, and himself were a lot more deserving of recognition.

Ben touched his arm. There was a hole in the sleeve of his shirt, and the dark stain around it was his blood. His arm was still tender from the bullet that had grazed it. How could they honor Trevor when Shank died to make sure the Resistance had food? They should honor Shank. Ben's dragonfire flared again and lit a bag of shaffs on fire. He grabbed an empty sack and beat it until it was out.

Ben left the storage room and went back to the dining hall. Dion was speaking. "Shank died making sure the trucks full of luka beans could get safely away. He is a hero, and we will not forget his sacrifice. Because of what he did, the Resistance can keep fighting."

The fire in Ben's belly had died down until he looked for Allison and found her standing nearby with Trevor. They had their arms around each other, and Trevor was wearing the cardboard crown. Fire exploded from Ben once more. He turned away, but not fast enough. When he turned back, Allison stood not far away, looking shocked and scared.

The left side of her face was red, and her left shirt sleeve scorched. The luka bean crown was on the ground in flames.

Ben was appalled; the last person he wanted to hurt was Allison. He was angry at himself, angry at Trevor, and angry at everyone except her. He also felt a deep sense of shame. He was supposed to have more control over his powers. He needed to have more control. A Dragonborn without it could do a great deal of damage. Allison took a step toward him with her hand outstretched. Ben could tell she was afraid of him, and it broke his heart. He couldn't bear the thought of trying to explain what had just happened, especially to her. There was no way to justify it without making himself look like a total dweeb. For the first time, he wondered why the Guardian had sent him when his life was so out of control.

Allison took two more tentative steps toward him. And then a few more. Trevor's hand was on her arm, and he was trying to hold her back. Ben turned and fled. He ran into one of the tunnels. Only those people assigned to a tunnel were supposed to enter them because of the dangers in each one, but at this point, Ben didn't care what the rules or the risks were. He needed to be alone. He kept flaring dragon fire so he could see in the dark. He kept going long after he stopped hearing sounds coming from the common area. Ben ran on until the tunnel ended. It might have gone further once upon a time, but it was now blocked by boulders and rock that had fallen from above.

He sat on one of the fallen boulders and leaned back against the tunnel wall. Tears were leaking from his eyes, which made him even angrier. Miss Templeton had said that little control over your emotions was a sign of the Wrathborn season. He had denied it was happening to him but now had to admit that it was. He replayed what had just happened in his mind, and one thing became clear. He had to let go of his jealousy of Trevor or of anyone else Allison chose to be with in the future. He had to do this not just for Allison's safety but for his own peace of mind.

He was sitting there quietly when he heard a voice. "I can't believe the Resistance lives underground like rats."

"The prisoner said they were underground. Besides, rats living with rats makes sense to me."

"People will say all kinds of things under torture."

"That's true, but I still think he was telling the truth. He said there was a tunnel under that old building, and there was."

"What did Commander Japeson think?"

"He didn't think it was likely, but he told me to check it out. He said he was going to report it to our great leader."

The voices sounded so close. At first, Ben thought they must be on the other side of the boulders that blocked the tunnel, but then he caught sight of a light shining through a crack in the tunnel wall and realized that the men must be in another tunnel that came close to the one he was in. As he listened, the voices started to fade away. Ben stood up and ran as fast as he could to warn the others. When he arrived in the common area, lunch was over, and most people had dispersed, but Mara sat with Dion and some of the other Resistance leaders at one of the tables. Ben ran directly to them. "Grek's men are in the tunnels," he said. "I heard them talking. They tortured someone who told them how to find you."

"Did they say anything else?" Mara asked.

"They've come through a tunnel entrance under an old building," Ben said.

"There are several that match that description. What else do you have?"

"It came close to the one that ends in a rockfall. The entrance on this end is second to the left," Ben said.

"That's the one on the corner of Bloom and Park," a fair-haired man said and then stood to his feet. "Something must have gone wrong with our monitoring system, or else they brought whoever they tortured with them."

Ben followed him to a group sitting in a circle at the far end of the large room. "Intruders in the Bloom Street tunnel," he said. Without another word, three people left the circle and went to get weapons.

"Any idea how many there were?" the fair-haired man asked Ben.

"I have no idea. I heard two voices, but there could have been more."

"My name is Keen by the way."

"Ben."

"Everyone knows your name," Keen said.

Ben wasn't sure whether that was a positive or a negative thing. Given what had just happened, Ben guessed it was negative.

"With any luck, Grek's men have blundered into a trap," Keen said. "But we need to make sure. They would have left someone at Bloom Street to watch their backs. Turk, I want you to take two others and deal with whoever is there. Stay there and make sure no one leaves." Turk left, and Ben assumed they were going through a tunnel that came out somewhere near Bloom and Park.

Keen led them into the same tunnel Ben had gone in earlier. Each of them, including Ben, took a helmet with a light down from a hook on the wall. Keen and the two men still with him took off at a run into the tunnel. When it diverged, Keen went left where Ben had gone to the right.

Keen stopped just before they reached a place where water covered the floor of the tunnel. "Pruit," he said. "There is a ledge under the water on the left side. Stay close to the wall. And don't lose your footing. You're a goner if you do. There is a hollowed-out place on the left wall about thirty paces in. Hide there until the intruders go past. You two, Ben and Geone, when I give the order, make sure the intruders see you and when they do turn and run. We want them to run after you." After giving those instructions, Keen pressed himself against the tunnel wall in a spot where he would be hard to see.

They didn't have long to wait before they saw the lights. There was a third man behind the first two who were walking side by side. The two men in front were talking, and Ben recognized their voices.

"Now," Keen said when the intruders were about twelve feet away.

Ben and Geone jumped into the middle of the tunnel. The two intruders in front didn't notice them at first because they were lost in conversation, but the man following them did. He yelled out a warning. As soon as the front two looked up, Ben and Geone turned and ran. A blast from a weapon hit the wall beside Ben, and shards of rock hit the side of his head. He stumbled forward but righted himself and ran faster.

Ben stopped and turned when he heard a shriek. There was no sign of the first two men. The third man had stopped running and was teetering beside the water that went across the pathway. While Ben watched, Pruit came out of his hiding place and pushed the man from behind. The man's hands grappled with the air before he disappeared.

"There's a stream of water under there," Geone said.

"The current is strong, and it pulls everything in. We don't know where it comes from or where it goes, but people who fall in are rarely seen again."

20. The Key

Charla knew what she needed to do, but she didn't know how to do it. She also didn't know if Mara would approve. She'd been adamant that Charla was just supposed to look around and then return. Charla didn't think they could take the time for the detailed planning Mara wanted to do, now that people knew the Resistance was living under the city. She thought about getting the key while Grek slept and using it to retrieve the Medallion, but what if something went wrong. There was too much at stake for Grek to catch her.

She'd taken the message out of Grek's in-box, but there would be other messages. It crossed her mind that the paper she carried in her pocket was so important that she should abandon everything else and return to the Resistance right away, but she didn't want to go through the pipe between the two fountains again. She wasn't sure she would survive a second trip. She needed a new way out of the palace. Besides, the mission to retrieve the Medallion was of primary importance. It would keep Grek from living on for many more years, perhaps hundreds more.

She wasn't sure what to do as she hid under the soiled napkin, but she knew the Resistance needed a copy of that key. It crossed her mind that she could go home with

Selina. Her instincts told her the serving girl would help her as long as it didn't put her own life in danger. Yet, she also knew Mara would disapprove of her taking the risk of revealing herself to Selina. She would also not approve of her making a plan and carrying it out on her own, but Mara wasn't here. She hadn't seen the way Selina smiled. There wasn't any time to waste now that people knew where to find the Resistance. Charla felt sure Selina would help her find something to use to make an impression of the key. But what if she was wrong? Charla didn't think she had a choice but to find out.

While they waited outside the elevator, she ran across the plate to Selina's hand because she'd noticed there was a fold in the sleeve of her uniform where she could hide. By the time the elevator door opened, she was safely hidden within the fold.

"Watch yourself," Selina said. "He's in a foul mood today."

"What's happened now?" asked a male voice Charla hadn't heard before.

Selina put the tray down on the counter. "The Resistance attacked several warehouses last night."

Whoever belonged to the new voice swore in words that did not translate into anything Charla recognized. "I wish

Grek would crush the Resistance once and for all," the man said. "They create no end of trouble for good, hard-working people."

Charla peeked out and saw that the night baker was gone, and in his place was the day cook who had dark well-groomed hair, a little goatee, and a clean, well-pressed uniform. One of Charla's questions was answered when a new serving woman with blond hair done up in a bun came through the kitchen door. Staff did arrive and depart through that door.

"Did you hear?" she asked while she took off her coat and hung it on a peg by the door.

"About the warehouses?" Selina asked.

"You did hear," the woman said. "Security is really tight. I was stopped twice by human guards, and my eyes were scanned several times by drones. That's why I'm late."

"That's a better excuse than the one you used yesterday," Selina muttered under her breath. Then she spoke more loudly. "It doesn't matter; his Excellency has just had his breakfast, so you might have a few hours before he or the Generals ring."

"Good." The woman sat on the chair Selina had been sitting on earlier. "I'll just try and catch up on some sleep until then."

Selina walked over to the door, took a jacket off a peg, slipped it on, and left the kitchen. Charla rearranged herself so she could see out from under the jacket while remaining hidden.

The courtyard outside the door was small and surrounded by a hedge except for a gate near the palace wall. The cat was sitting on the bench, licking its paws. Selina stopped to pet the cat before walking to the gate and opening it. A guard stood on the other side. Selina hesitated and then stepped through.

Charla heard the sound of a slap and watched as Selina's hand clenched. She thought she knew what had just happened. The guard had slapped Selina on the behind as she walked through the gate. Charla was certain of it when Selina mumbled "fart sauce" a few steps further on.

There were more soldiers in the square than there had been the day before, and several more drones were flying through the air. On the screens around the square was a new video focused on families. The message was that these families owed their happiness to Grek. Interspersed with repeats of that video was a message that there would be food shortages thanks to the Resistance and a reminder that there was a reward for the capture of any of the following people. Faces of Resistance members flashed on the screen.

The soldiers seemed to know who Selina was and left her alone, but the drones kept flying by to scan her eyes. She kept walking as the drones scanned. They flew backward in front of her face to stay in position. She was questioned by a guard for the first time when she waited for the people mover. He wanted to know where she'd been and whether she'd seen anything strange.

The people mover was full, so Selina stood in front of the seats holding onto an overhead bar. It gave Charla a view of the city underneath them. She watched as they left the city center behind and traveled through an area of dilapidated and crumbling buildings. The people on the streets looked poor and beaten down. Selina did not get off until they arrived in an area with a mixture of old and new buildings. Some people on the streets looked poor, while others wore clothing that suggested they were prosperous but not wealthy. After walking two blocks, they arrived at Selina's apartment on the third floor of an older walk-up.

Unfortunately, Selina did not live alone. A man was waiting for her. Charla hadn't thought about the possibility that she might not be able to reveal herself to Selina privately when they arrived at her apartment. The presence of another person complicated things. It increased the risk she was taking by revealing herself. It didn't take her long to realize the man in the apartment was not Selina's husband, as she first assumed, but her brother, whose name was Brent.

Brent was looking out the window. "What's going on? There have been sirens all night."

"The Resistance attacked some storage facilities and made off with a lot of food," Selina responded.

"I told you that would happen after the prison escape. I just didn't think it would happen so fast."

"Apparently, neither did Grek," Selina said. "He wasn't ready for them. The cook's brother is with the city guard, and he said they were getting ready to put extra guards on all the food storage places starting today."

"Ha, this news has made my day," Brent said.

"It might mean food shortages for all of us." Selina sat on a chair in the living room and undid the laces on her shoes. Charla took that opportunity to climb out of the cuff on Selina's uniform and hide behind the leg of the chair she was sitting on.

"I don't care," Brent said. "I wish I was with the Resistance instead of hiding out in this apartment. You're still trying to find out how I can join them, aren't you? You'd tell me if you heard something, wouldn't you?"

"I would tell you. It's not easy to go around trying to find out how to get in touch with the Resistance without raising the suspicions of the wrong people."

"I should just go out and see if I can find them."

"You know you can't go out on the street, not unless you want to be scooped up and put in jail for not showing up at the military recruitment center when they called your name."

"It would be a change of scenery, and I wouldn't be sitting here eating up your rations."

"Don't say that, Brent. You know how much you mean to me. If they catch you and you refuse to join, you'll end up in a concentration camp where they'll work you to death. Besides, it's not so bad. The baker always gives me a little food to take home."

Charla stepped out from behind the chair leg and grew in size. "If you want to meet the Resistance, I may be able to help."

Selina jumped up from the chair she was sitting on, and Brent picked it up and raised it over his head to use as a weapon. Charla held her hands in front of her to show them that there was nothing in them.

Brent slowly lowered the chair. "Who are you? And how did you get in here?"

"My name is Charla, and I'm a chosen of the Guardian."

"I've never heard of the Guardian," Brent said. "Who or what is that."

"The full title is Guardian of the Six Worlds. This is one of the worlds in the Guardian care. I have been sent from another world to help you."

"Come on!" Selina exclaimed. "That's unbelievable."

"You expect us to believe that?" Brent asked.

Charla didn't bother arguing. She sat down on the chair Brent had placed back down on the ground and transformed her legs into a tail. She breathed in relief as soon as she did so and decided to remain seated as a mermaid.

Selina grabbed a chair for herself and sat in it. "How did you do that?"

"It's natural for me." Charla lifted her Mer tail from where it rested on the ground. "There are a few people in my world who can transform their tails into human legs. I'm ashamed to say that Grek was originally from my world, and he can do this too."

"That's unbelievable." Brent looked from Charla to his sister. "We would know, wouldn't we?"

"Some of us are trained to fit into other worlds."

"You say Grek can do this too." Selina pointed at Charla's tail. "Is that why he has a pool that he swims in every day and eats mostly raw fish?"

Charla nodded.

"Do you know, sometimes he even sleeps inside the pool?" Selina said.

"I didn't know, but it makes sense," Charla said.

"How did you get here?" Selina asked.

"I came home with you."

"How…" Selina's mouth hung open as Charla shrank in size and then grew again.

Brent grabbed hold of the nearby table the moment Charla began to shrink. "How is it possible for you to do that?

"It's a long story that involves the Guardian. I'll tell you how it works later, but, at the moment, I need your help," Charla said. "The Resistance needs your help."

"What do you think we can do for you?" Selina asked.

"I need a copy of the key that hangs around Grek's neck."

"What for? 'Brent asked.

"I need the key to open the locked door to where the Guardian's Medallion is kept."

"What's that, and why do you need it?" Selina asked.

"The Medallion is what has kept Grek alive far past his normal life span. If we can take away the Medallion, then he will die like any other normal person."

"I've heard rumors that Grek is centuries old," Brent said. "I assumed it was just a crazy story."

"Rather than trying to steal the key, I want to make a copy of it while Grek is asleep. I'm here because I hope you'll help me."

"Why would you think that?" Selina asked.

"I saw you wipe away the smile that came to your lips when you heard about the raids. I'm not wrong, am I? You don't support Grek and might be willing to help the Resistance."

"You're not wrong," Brent said. "How can we help?"

"I need wax or tree gum or something to make an impression of the key to take to the Resistance so they can make a duplicate."

Selina and Brent looked at each other with a puzzled look on their faces.

"We've never heard of either wax or tree gum."

"Something else then. Something we can press a key into and make an impression."

Selina and Brent sat in silence for a moment, then Brent spoke. "What about the dough mom used to make for us to play with when we were children. Do you think that would work?" It hardens reasonably quickly and keeps its shape.

"I think it just might," Selina said. "But we would need to figure out a way to keep it from getting wet."

"I have a waterproof bag," Charla said. "But it wouldn't hurt to have something else which would provide extra protection."

Brent stood and walked to the cupboard, where he pulled out a clear jar with a lid. "The only thing is," he said as he put it down on the table. "I don't want my sister taking risks."

"I'll be the only one taking whatever risks are needed," Charla said. "All Selina needs to do is drop me off in Grek's rooms before he goes to sleep and pick me up in the morning so she can take me with her when she leaves."

"I'll do it," Selina said. "Brent, you're not the only one in this family who wants to help the Resistance. I've gotten to know Grek by serving his food, and I want him gone more than anyone. He is a horrible man."

"Are you sure?" Brent furrowed his brow. "There might be more risk than we are aware of." He chewed his bottom lip.

Selina reached out and touched her brother's hand.

"Don't worry. I'll be fine. I'll get the recipe from Alba Bligh. Then you can make it while Charla and I sleep."

Brent nodded his head, and Selina left the apartment. He turned to Charla. "Promise that you will protect my sister."

"I will do everything I can to keep her safe."

"I would appreciate it if you put me in touch with the Resistance."

"I'll do what I can. I'll give them your contact information and tell them you'd like to join."

21. Back to the Palace

Selina carried Charla back into the palace in her pocket. She was more afraid than she thought she would be. Traveling on the people mover, she considered what it would mean if she got caught. At the very least, it would be the end of a job that was easy and paid well. She would be lucky if she didn't end up in prison or dead. And yet, not doing what she thought was right didn't feel like an option.

Grek was exploiting tribal identities that hadn't mattered for centuries. Friends were now enemies because their ancestors were part of a different tribe. Neighbors were finding fault with people they'd lived peacefully beside for years. In some places, it had erupted in violence. She knew she'd gotten the job in the palace not just for her ability but for her heritage. Anyone who asked too many questions and pointed out that things were not changing for the better risked ending up in a concentration camp. The security forces had taken Selina's favorite cousin and a friend. She hadn't seen them since.

Selina was determined not to see someone as her enemy simply because their family came from the east rather than the west. Selina was afraid that if she didn't do what she could, she might never have another chance to make a difference. Selina didn't want to go to her grave, thinking she might have been able to help bring change, but things stayed the same because she was afraid to act. She was equally fearful of becoming acclimatized to situations as they were and coming to the place of thinking injustice was normal.

Selina was annoyed with Brent. He wanted to keep her safe while getting involved himself. But sometimes, being safe wasn't an option you could live with. Yes, there was a risk, but not taking part would leave her with a lifetime of regret if Grek remained in power. She knew he would continue to stoke the flames of hate and division.

When they got to the palace grounds, Selina held her breath, waiting to see who was guarding the gate into the back garden. There were a couple of guards that made her life miserable. She suspected they did that to every young woman just because they could. When she caught sight of the guard who was at the gate, her breath caught in her throat. It was the worst of the guards, the one who would often insist on a kiss before he would let her pass. She usually found a way to avoid kissing him. What she sometimes did was make sure she got there before the baker did. She would wait for him by the people mover so they could walk in together, but she knew that the baker would have arrived by now. Sometimes she chatted up one of the friendly guards and asked him to walk in with her, but she didn't see any guards she knew.

"Hello, sweet cakes," the guard drawled. "Today is the day. You are going to kiss me. You know you want to. You've just been teasing me by saying no. It's time to stop being a tease."

"Geo, I don't want to kiss you, and I never will want to," Selina spoke in a louder than normal voice.

"It's time to stop playing hard to get," Geo said. "One kiss, that's all it'll take. There's such magic in my kisses. Kiss me once, and you'll never be able to get enough of me."

Selina tried to step around Geo, but he grabbed hold of her right arm. She struggled to free herself, but he just tightened his grip. Geo was so much stronger; she couldn't resist the pull into his embrace. He slipped his arm around her waist and pulled her toward him, so their bodies were touching. His right hand held Selina's arm not far from where Charla hid in her pocket. Geo moved his lips toward Selina's, but she turned her head aside before he reached them. After Geo tried several times to kiss her without success, he squeezed her arm hard enough to cause Selina to cry out in pain.

Charla saw Geo's fingers tighten and dig into Selina's arm. She decided she had to do something. She grew so that her upper body was out of Selina's pocket. She hoped

Geo would not look down and see her. Charla pulled out her knife. The more she grew, the larger it became. Right now, it was the size of a pin, but sharper. Charla reached out to slice Geo's hand, but it was still too far away. So, she grew even more. At this size, she had to hold onto Selina's jacket with one hand to keep from falling out. Charla raised the knife and sliced it across the fleshy area between Geo's thumb and index finger. She was still slicing when she began to shrink. Geo howled and let go of Selina's arm. Charla caught sight of a thin line of blood before her head disappeared inside the pocket. Selina pushed past him and ran into the courtyard to the kitchen door. She opened it and flung herself through, closing the door and leaning against it. Her breath was ragged as she wiped away tears from her eyes.

"You're late," the night baker said.

"I'm sorry, Deffon. The guard stopped me and wouldn't let me through the gate."

"That same guard has caused problems for you before. I think he might be sweet on you."

Selina snorted.

"He's good looking, and he's got a good job. You could do a lot worse."

"I'm not interested in Geo and never will be. He disgusts me. Besides, I think he has a wife."

"In the old days, I could have complained about his behavior, but those who command the guards no longer seem to have the high standards they used to. One of the problems with corruption at the top is that it doesn't stay there. They replace good with those who have no integrity. If I complained, they might just come up with some trumped-up story to get both of us fired. It's a sad day when corruption is so pervasive."

Selina looked at the baker in surprise. He had never said anything like this before. Clearly, he was not a Grek fan. "Don't risk your job for me," she said. "We can only hope that something will happen to change the leadership so that truth will matter again.

"Grek has already called down for his tea and fish. I was going to take it up myself if you didn't get here in the next few minutes."

"What happened to Mina?" Selina asked. The woman who covered the day shift should still be in the kitchen.

"She had to leave early. One of her children is sick."

"I'm glad you waited for me. I wouldn't want Grek asking where we were. It might get both Mina and me in trouble."

"Here's the tray." Deffon picked it up and put it down on her side of the counter. "You'd better hurry. He'll already be wondering what happened to it."

Selina put her bag down and took off her jacket. She hung them over the back of the chair, but before she did, she carefully reached into the left pocket of her coat and picked Charla up. With the Mer girl hidden in her closed hand, Selina walked over to the counter. She lifted the napkin, placed Charla underneath it, then picked up the tray and headed for the elevator. Monitors watched the elevators and hallways, so they agreed not to say anything as they traveled from the kitchen to Grek's residence and office.

When they stood outside the door, Selina dropped the handkerchief she was carrying, and in the process of picking it up, put Charla down on the ground. She opened the door and went through it with the miniature Mer girl following at her heels.

The plan was for Charla to spend the night in Grek's rooms. Selina would pick her up in the morning. Hopefully, she would have made an impression of the key in the dough Brent had made by then.

Selina had told Charla where Grek slept, so she went straight there, making sure to keep hidden as much as possible as she walked across the large reception area. Grek was sitting on a recliner in that room with his lower body raised by the footrest. A heavy blanket covered his bottom half to keep it hidden. Charla guessed that he didn't want people to know about his ability to transform into a Mer.

When she got to the bedroom, Charla hid underneath a dresser. From there, she looked around. A door stood open, leading into a large washroom. She could see an oversized bathtub and thought how nice it would be to soak in it. She was feeling somewhat water-starved. As a Mer, she needed to spend time in the water every week, preferably every day. She wished she'd asked to bathe at Selina's house.

She didn't need to wait too long for Grek to arrive. He walked into the bedroom and closed the door behind him before disappearing into the bathroom. He was there for at least a half-hour. When he came out, his hair was wet, and he had removed the contacts in his eyes that made them look human.

He didn't have a bed so much as a sleeping platform. He took the chain with the key off of his neck and laid it on the table beside the bed. Charla was glad to see that he took it off. She was afraid he might sleep with it.

Grek lay down, and his legs transformed into a tail. Merpeople can tolerate a wide range of temperatures, so he did not need to sleep with any blankets, but he pulled one over his tail to hide it. He did lay his head upon a pillow. He lay on the bed for a few minutes but seemed to grow agitated. Finally, he got off the sleeping platform and went to the corner behind the door leading into the reception area. He picked up a long walking stick and swung it around the room with all his might. He went around the room several times, poking it into the corners and into the closet. He swung it high, and he swung it low. Then he went into the bathroom and did the same thing there. When he finished, he retraced his steps in the bedroom—swinging the stick this way and that. When he stopped, his face was red, and he was breathing hard. He climbed back onto his sleeping platform but did not put the walking stick back where he'd found it. Instead, he lay it on the platform beside him.

Charla remained hidden under the desk, confused as to why Grek had behaved so strangely. Then it hit her. He still had enough of the Guardian's special abilities to sense that something was not right. He sensed there was something in the room that didn't belong. Perhaps he even knew there was someone here. He circled the room, swinging the walking stick to catch a Chosen of the Guardian who might be invisible.

Charla wondered if he knew about the shrinking gift. Lea Waterborn said she'd never seen it before. Perhaps Grek had never seen it before either. If he knew about it, what would he do to find her? She had just asked herself that question when Grek got out of bed. This time he headed right to where she was with the walking stick in his hand. He must have been concentrating hard on finding the hidden presence. He came directly to where she was and swiped his hand across the top of the dresser. Then he took the stick and poked underneath it. When there was no contact, he got down on the ground and looked. By then,

Charla had moved so she was between the dresser leg and the wall.

"Nothing," Grek said. "I could have sworn there was something there." He dropped the stick off in the corner before climbing onto his sleeping platform again.

It was clear to Charla that he had never heard of the gift of shrinking in size. She decided to be sure Grek was asleep before making a move. She had no choice but to grow in size if she wanted to get hold of the key. If Grek opened his eyes while she was close to full size, it would be the end. Not only would she not be able to get a copy of the key, but she wouldn't be able to warn the Resistance that Grek would soon know where they were. She wished she'd given that information to Brent and told him to go to the square outside the palace and look for a man wearing a luka bean hat. She stayed where she was and watched Grek toss and turn. He got up and went into the washroom a couple of times during the night, but each time he'd picked up the key and taken it with him. She stayed awake through the night, watching for an opportunity. Her eyes were getting heavy. A couple of times, they closed in sleep, but only for a few minutes.

The sun was about to rise when Grek got out of bed and went to the washroom. The previous two times, he'd put the chain with the key on it around his neck. This time he forgot.

As soon as the bathroom door closed, Charla took out the container with the dough in it, grew to her full size, grabbed the key, and took an impression. She quickly wiped the key off and put it back down as close as she could to the way it was before. She had almost shrunk down to the size of a housefly when the bathroom door burst open. Grek raced across the floor and picked up the key. He stood there for a moment holding it as if he sensed something had changed.

Charla had flung herself to the floor and crawled under the nightstand as she continued to shrink. When Grek moved to the closet and took out a shirt, she noticed he had placed the key around his neck. He opened the bedroom door and went out. Charla went to the door and watched what he would do next. He went over to a black box attached to the wall and pushed a button. "Send up my breakfast," Grek demanded. Then he went into his office.

Charla breathed a sigh of relief. She had been afraid Grek would stay in bed longer than the day before, and Selina would not be the server on duty when he woke up. She had spent some time considering how she could wake him up if that appeared to be the case. However, he had actually gotten up earlier than the day before.

When the door opened, and Selina came in, Charla was waiting beside it. On their prearranged agreement, Selina dropped a napkin close to the table. Charla climbed under it, then Selina bent over and picked up the napkin. She carefully folded it up and put it in her pocket.

When they got back to the kitchen, Selina asked Deffon if he needed any help. When he said no, she sat in her chair to wait for the shift change. The day cook arrived an hour and a half later.

"I'll walk you out," Deffon said. "I think you can leave now even though Mina is not here yet. She should be here any minute."

Selina felt a great deal of gratitude to the night baker. The guards wouldn't bother her if she was with him.

However, it might be difficult to pass Charla onto the street cleaner wearing the luka bean hat. If she said no, it would be the first time, and he would find it strange that she would not want his protection. She came up with an idea that would not make Deffon suspicious. She just hoped the street cleaner was young and relatively handsome.

She was thrilled the night baker had waited when she discovered that the guard who had stopped her the night before was still on duty. She wondered if that was why Mina was late. Did she wait until the shift changed to come to the gate? No other guard was as terrible as this one.

Perhaps she wasn't the only one he insisted on getting a kiss from. The guard scowled at her and pursed his lips as if kissing her. She shuddered and looked away.

There were other guards at the front of the palace, but none of them had ever been a serious bother. Some of them had quietly whistled as she walked by, but she could handle that.

She looked around the square for a cleaner with a yellow hat. She found one sweeping the courtyard nearby. His back was to her, so she couldn't see what he looked like. The good thing was Deffon couldn't see either.

"Thank you so much, Deffon. I was afraid of walking past that guard this morning. I'll be okay now. I see my boyfriend, and I need to ask him something."

"I didn't know you were dating."

"I don't tell you quite everything," Selina said with a forced laugh. "Although the truth is, we haven't been going out very long."

As she walked toward the man with the yellow hat, Selina put her hand in her pocket. The napkin was still there, and so was Charla. She took it out of her pocket with Charla cradled inside and walked to the man. "Excuse me," she said behind his back. "I think I have something you're looking for." The man in the yellow hat turned and looked at her. He was young and good looking, but his hat said, 'life is meant to be lived.'

Selina stepped back and put the napkin back into her pocket. "I'm sorry," she said. "I thought you were someone else."

She turned away. There at the fountain was another cleaner wearing a yellow hat. She hadn't seen him before because he'd been hidden behind the fountain when the water was flowing. Now that it was off, he was visible. She walked over as quickly as she could. This time she made sure to read the words on his hat before speaking. "'Life does go better with Luka Beans. 'It's good that the Resistance found some," she said quietly.

He stepped back, clearly shocked, but then smiled and leaned toward her. "Life does indeed go better with Luka Beans."

"I have something for you," Selina said quietly. "Hold it with care as it is breakable." She took the napkin out of her pocket and gave it to the cleaner. Then she kissed him on the lips. "I told the fellow I work with that you are my boyfriend."

"Wish I was," he said as he slipped the napkin into his pocket. Then he gently kissed Selina. "Just to make it more realistic," he said. He smiled, and she smiled tentatively back. Then she turned and quickly walked toward the people mover.

22. A Plan is Made

Mort, the street cleaner, finished the hour that remained on his shift before carrying Charla back to the Resistance headquarters. With great care, he took her out of his pocket. She started to grow while still in his hand.

"Charla, I was beginning to worry about you," Mara said. "Did you find out anything that will help us?"

"There are about a dozen off-world Chosen in prison at Fairhaven. The Medallion is in a locked vault in the middle of a pool connected to Grek's private rooms. The vault can only be reached by swimming through a tunnel system that wraps itself around the island several times. Grek has made it so only a Mer can get there. In addition, the box is locked."

The people gathered around Charla stared at each other in silence.

"Well, we knew it wasn't going to be easy," Mara said, then looked up at Charla. "You did well. Very well."

"You may not have that long," Charla said and then handed Mara the message she had taken out of Grek's inbox. "Presumably, whoever sent this will send another if they don't get a response."

Mara read the message and then passed it on to Dion. "We had three men come and check out the tunnel," she said to Charla. "It's possible they were the only ones who knew, but I doubt it. I don't think we can take the chance. We've been discussing where to go from here. We haven't come up with anything that keeps us together and safe.

"This letter tells me we need to move now," Dion said, "Maybe even tonight." She passed the letter on to Jupe.

"You said the Medallion is kept in a locked vault that only a Mer can get to," Mara said. "It's a good thing we have a Mer on our side then."

"Does it open with an eye scan?" Jupe asked.

"No. Grek has a key around his neck."

"That's rather old-fashioned of him," Dion said.

"But very helpful for us," Mara said.

Charla reached into the bag that hung over her shoulder and pulled out the jar. Selina had given her some soft fluffy material, so the dough wouldn't bang against the hard sides of the jar as she traveled. She took the mold out, carefully unwrapped it, and held it out to Mara. "Do you think you can use this impression to make a copy of the key?"

Mara immediately turned to a nearby woman and placed the mold Charla had made in her hands. "You know what to do," she said.

"You've done extremely well, Charla. Did you also manage to find another way into the palace?"

"I found a way in for Ben and myself."

"Why just you and Ben?" Dion asked.

"We're the only ones who can shrink. I enlisted the help of a server in the palace. She's willing to carry us back in. Her brother wants to join the Resistance."

"How did you find that out?" Mara asked.

"I saw her smile when Grek spoke about the Resistance. I didn't know what else to do, so I went home with her. I wouldn't have revealed myself to them, but she and her brother spoke about their desire to help the Resistance."

Mara frowned. "It was risky to involve someone else, but I guess we don't have time to play it safe."

"Perhaps now is also the time to come out of the shadows and take our fight directly to Grek," Jupe said as he passed the letter on to Trevor, who was standing next to him.

"Perhaps it is," Mara said.

"What would happen if you attacked the palace?" Trevor asked. "Would soldiers be pulled away from Truehaven to defend it?

"Very likely," Mara responded.

"This is what I think we should do then," Trevor said.

"We should start by getting Charla and Ben into the palace with the help of the serving girl and her brother. We should try to get them in tonight if the key can be ready by then."

"It can be," Mara said.

"Then, sometime early tomorrow we should attack the palace. Following the palace's attack, a smaller force should attack Truehaven after first waiting for the troops stationed there to leave. I'm guessing some of them will go to help defend the palace. If they don't leave by mid-morning, attack anyway. With any luck, we will rescue the Chosen and take control of Truehaven so it can be the new home for the Resistance. It will bring you out into the open, but I think it is what you need to do."

"But," Dion said, "he will know where we are and send everything he has to attack us."

"That's true," Trevor said. "But if we control Truehaven, we control the portal. The Guardian can send other Chosen through it without them getting arrested right away."

Mara made a gesture asking people to refrain from speaking. She closed the eye not covered by a patch and rested her chin on her hand. She stood in silence for close to a minute before opening her eye. "Truehaven is very defendable. Grek might know where we are, but he'll have a hard time dislodging us from there. I say we do what Trevor suggests."

"We should take all our supplies with us because we won't be able to come back here for them," Jupe jumped in, his voice excited. "I also think we should make a plan to break into the place where they broadcast Grek's video's and see if we can replace them with one of our own."

"I agree," Dion said. "There are good people out there who need to know they are not alone in resisting what Grek is doing. Some of them will join us if they have the opportunity. Who knows how many, like the two willing to help Charla, are just waiting for an opportunity?"

Charla broke into the conversation. "Selina's brother Brent worked there. He'll be able to help."

"Perfect," Mara said.

The conversation continued, but in the end, they agreed to do what Trevor suggested. Mort would carry Ben and Charla to Selina's house. He liked the idea of continuing to be Selina's pretend boyfriend.

"Okay, Mara said. "I know we've just moved the luka beans and other supplies down to this location, but now I want it all carried back up to the warehouse. Everything needs to be ready to go by tonight.

Dion was given command of the attack on Truehaven. Trevor was assigned to be her second in command. When the meeting broke up, Trevor turned to Dion and asked a question. "Is there a way for us to get our hands on the uniforms the soldiers wear?"

"We already have them," she said. "They've come in handy a few times."

"Could we get hold of the kind of vehicles they use to take prisoners out there?" he asked.

"We certainly can," Dion said.

Charla had fallen asleep during the discussion. Jared picked her up and took her to one of the rooms lined with bunkbeds. He gently laid her on one, and she slept until he came and woke her up later in the afternoon. "The key is ready, and it's almost time for you to go," he said.

Mort stood in front of Selina's door and felt his pulse quicken. He was looking forward to seeing her again. He rang the bell, but it wasn't Selina who answered. It was her brother, still in his pajamas.

"Is Selina here?" Mort asked. "Please tell Selina her boyfriend has arrived."

The brother stared at him for a minute, then quickly pulled him into the apartment. Once the door was closed, he called out. "Selina, your friend from the palace square is here. The life is better with luka beans, guy."

"I'll be there in a minute," Selina called out from somewhere inside the apartment.

Mort reached into his pockets and gently lifted Charla and Ben out, one in each hand. He sat them on their own chairs and stood back. By the time Selina came out, they were both full-sized.

"We were wondering if you would carry my friend and me back into the palace," Charla said.

"Of course, I'll be ready to leave in a half-hour," Selina said.

"Mort is going to escort you," Charla said. "He'll continue the charade of being your boyfriend to help you get safely past the guard."

"Thank you," Selina said, smiling shyly at Mort.

Mort smiled back. "It is my pleasure." He paused. "You know I'll have to kiss you goodbye when we get to the gate."

"Of course," Selina said. "We need to make it look real."

"The key is ready, and Ben and I need to get into Grek's chambers," Charla continued.

Selina hesitated for a moment. "If you get caught, please don't tell anyone about how I helped you."

"We're not going to be captured," Charla said. "But if we are, I promise we won't tell anyone how we got in."

"Brent," Mort said. "Charla said you were an electronics expert with knowledge of the communications system."

"It was my specialty in college, and I worked at the broadcasting center until Grek came to power, then I quit. I just couldn't stand creating propaganda for him."

"If you are serious about joining the Resistance, we need your help," Mort continued. "We want you to help us use the communications system to our advantage."

"I'm willing to do anything I can to stop Grek."

"In that case, a young woman will come by in a little while and take you to a place where people are gathering to discuss how to infiltrate Grek's communication center and replace his messages with one of our own. But before you agree, be aware that you could be putting your life in danger."

"Of course, I'll do it," Brent said. "I've been waiting for an opportunity like this for a long time."

Mort took his 'Life is better with Luka Beans 'hat off and gave it to Brent. "Wear this. Our people don't know you. This will tell them that you are one of us. If anyone asks, tell them Mort gave it to you."

23. Back to the Palace

An hour and a half later, Ben and Charla were in Grek's private quarters, hiding behind a table in their miniature form. They were waiting for some indication that the assault on the palace had started when Grek's phone rang.

He listened for a moment, then said, "Send them down." In a few minutes, two men in military uniforms entered. Grek directed them to sit at the conference table.

"You have a reason for wanting to see me?" he asked.

"A couple of days ago, we sent a message that a prisoner, under interrogation, confessed that the Resistance was living under the city. We sent three men to check it out. They haven't returned. We've also checked back through our records. There have been other claims that the Resistance was under the city, but no one took it seriously until now. We sent someone over to the town planning office. They gave us the name of an old man who retired from city planning. We sent someone over to see him. He told us there are abandoned sewage tunnels under the city. It is one of the reasons nothing was built where the park is. There are tunnels everywhere, but there are more under the park than anywhere else. He thought it highly unlikely, but not impossible, that people were living underneath the park.

He knew of some entry points to get into the old sewage system. The notes from previous interrogations produced one more so that we have four places to check out, including the one the three men disappeared into. We have teams ready to go with your approval."

Grek tapped his fingers on the desk. "First, I want you to bomb the park. Hit it with the biggest bomb we have."

"But our biggest bomb will flatten some of the nearby buildings. People will be hurt."

"Some of them will die," Grek said. "That's what happens when you drop a bomb."

"Are you suggesting we shouldn't clear the park first?" one of the men asked.

"If we start clearing the park, we'll warn the Resistance."

"But there are all kinds of street vendors and families who gather there, not to mention the shoppers." The man's voice became louder and higher, and a bead of sweat broke out on his forehead.

"We all need to die sometime," Grek said. Those words, coming from a man who had lived several centuries more than a normal person and who had rebelled against the Guardian to live several more centuries, made Charla's blood boil.

The same man tried again to point out that this was not a wise thing to do. "You'll make people angry. You'll lose support if you do this."

"No," Grek said. "I can't control the actions of rogue pilots who sympathize with the Resistance. The only thing I can do is make sure they pay for their crimes. You will shoot the pilot out of the air before they land."

The two soldiers looked at each other. It was clear they wanted to object but hoped the other person would risk angering their boss. The oldest one spoke first. "We may have trouble finding a pilot willing to drop a bomb on a park filled with people."

Grek leaned forward and stared at them. "Choose who you ask to do this well, and promise them ten thousand credits when their mission is complete. Some people will kill their grandmother for that much money," Grek paused, then added. "If you are not willing to carry out my orders, I'll find someone who will. You are both being paid well enough not to question what I tell you to do."

"Could we at least wait until later tonight?" the older man asked. There was sweat on his brow, and he was visibly shaken. He stuttered as he continued to speak. "The families will have gone home by then to put their children to bed."

Grek flung out his arm, and lightning struck the older soldier square in the chest. He flopped over and fell on the floor. Grek leaned forward and looked at the remaining officer. "Do you have any objections to carrying out my plan?"

"No," the man said, his voice shaking. "I'll do exactly what you commanded."

"On second thought, I'd like to change the plan. You can do it tomorrow morning, but I want there to be people in the park."

"Of course, your Excellency," the soldier said.

"Send someone down to carry out the trash," Grek growled. After the soldier left, he got up and went into his office.

"I never realized he still had some powers," Ben whispered.

Charla was silent. She was too stunned by what she'd seen. Finally, she spoke, "We need to warn the Resistance."

"They're planning to leave anyway," Ben said.

"But what if something delays them. I need to stay here since I'm the only one with any hope of getting to the Medallion, but you need to go and warn them."

"All right," Ben said. "But don't take any unnecessary risks. Unless you have a really clear path, wait until I get back."

There was a knock on the door. Two soldiers came in and picked up the body of the dead man. Ben followed them out of Grek's quarters. He had to run to keep up with them. He was disappointed when they walked past the elevator toward the heavy metal door guarded by a soldier at the end of the hall. Ben was unsure how to get back to the kitchen when the elevator door opened and a man came out. He also turned toward the heavy doors. Ben jumped into the elevator before the door closed completely. When it did, he grew in size until he could push the button that would take the elevator up to the main floor, then he quickly shrunk back down in size. From what Ben understood, every area of the palace was monitored. He just hoped that whoever did so was looking at something else for the few seconds it took him to grow and shrink.

When the door opened, Ben ran to the kitchen. Selina was helping the night baker make sweet cakes. Ben wondered how he could get her attention without being seen. He grew in size and was reaching out to touch her ankle when the cat attacked him. It came from behind and pinned him down on the ground; a sharp claw dug into his shoulders. When it looked like the cat was going to eat him, Ben did the only thing he could do. He grew even larger.

"What's going on over there?" Deffon asked. He couldn't see Ben from where he stood across the counter from Selina.

"The cat has some…" Selina stopped talking when she saw what the cat had. She grabbed it by the scruff of its neck to make it let go of Ben.

"What does the cat have?" Deffon started to walk around the counter to see for himself. Fortunately, it was a long counter with two double sinks in the middle.

Selina managed to get the cat to let go of Ben, and as soon as she did, he shrunk in size again. She picked him up and held him gently inside her closed hand while Deffon picked up the cat. She put Ben in her pocket as Deffon walked to the door and put the cat outside.

Shortly after that, Selina casually mentioned that she needed to go to the washroom. When the door was closed and locked, she put Ben on the counter so he could grow. "I'm sorry about this. It was the only place I could think of where we were guaranteed time alone. What's happened? Is Charla okay?"

Ben explained how they had heard the plan to bomb the park and decided he had to warn the Resistance, so they weren't underground when the bombs fell.

Selina was appalled by what she heard. She knew from her personal experience with him that Grek was a terrible man, but it was hard to believe even he would do something so dreadful. "I don't think you should go. You need to be here to help Charla. I'll go, but you have to tell me where."

"That's the problem, I don't know where to tell you to go, and I don't want to ask you to take the risk. I'm going to speak to a man in the park who I believe is part of the resistance, but I don't know for sure. He has a 'Life is Better with Luka Beans 'booth and wears the same hat that Mort wears.

"I know something about that booth, but what is it?" Selina asked herself. "What makes you think he's part of the Resistance?"

"There's the hat, and then the way he and Dion seemed to know each other."

"That's not a lot to go on."

"I know, that's why I'd rather risk my own life rather than yours."

"Let's go together," Selina said. "I can get you there faster than you can get there on your own. You can approach him while I watch. Then if he blows the whistle on you, I'll look for a way to get you out of there and if I can't, I'll try to find a way to contact the Resistance and warn them."

Ben stared at Selina for a moment, then nodded.

Selina was partway through the kitchen when she remembered what she knew about the luka bean booth in the park. She stopped walking and turned toward the night baker. "Deffon, do I remember correctly that your son owns a booth in the park?"

"He does," Deffon said.

"What's the name of it?"

"Life goes better with Luka Beans. He's trying to sell an iced dessert made of beans. Personally, I think it's nasty, but he assures me he has a loyal clientele."

"Is it possible his booth is a cover for his involvement with the Resistance?" Selina could imagine Ben's shock at hearing her say those words, but he didn't know Deffon.

Her words shocked Deffon as well. His mouth fell open, and his eyes went wide, then he bowed his head. "Of course," he whispered to himself. "Why didn't I see it before?" He lifted his head and stared hard at Selina. "Why are you asking that question?"

"I have learned that Grek plans to bomb the park because he believes the Resistance is underground in that spot."

"Are they?"

"I have reason to believe they are."

"But surely, Grek will clear the park before it's bombed."

"From what I understand, he doesn't plan to do that. He plans to bomb the park and blame it on the Resistance. I want to leave the kitchen so that I can warn them about his plan. And before you ask, I'm not part of the Resistance, but lately, I've come into contact with them."

"I supported Grek when he first came to power. I was wrong, and my son was right. Gabe saw the danger right from the start." Deffon shook his head. "Promise me that you will warn my son. I asked him not to have anything to do with the Resistance, but now I believe he didn't listen."

"I will warn him and hope he'll warn the Resistance," Selina said as she walked toward the door.

"Wait! How are you planning to get there?" Deffon asked.

"By people mover."

"Too slow. Take a cab. I'll transfer some credits to your account to help you pay for it. There will be one waiting at the corner. I'll walk you out, so you don't have any problem with the guard."

They were in the park ten minutes later. The cab driver was confused when they left. One person had entered his vehicle and two left it. Selina and Ben wandered through the vendors looking for the one selling an iced dessert made of luka beans. They would have made better progress if they hadn't had to stop and kiss so often to prevent a drone from seeing Ben's eyes.

They found Gabe's booth on the outskirts of the park. There was no one at his cart when they reached it, but he arrived shortly after that.

"Hello Gabe, my name is Ben, and I was with Dion when we came through the park a couple of days ago. I was one of the escaping prisoners."

Gabe opened his mouth as if to yell for one of the guards who stood around in the park.

Selina put her hand on his arm. "Please don't, I work with your father Deffon," she said quickly. "He sent us to you. Perhaps he's mistaken, but he thought you might be part of the Resistance."

"What makes you think that?" Gabe asked.

"You're wearing a 'Life is better with Luka Beans hat,'" Ben said. "The only other person I know with a hat like that is named Mort."

"You know Mort and Dion?" Gabe asked.

"Yes," Ben said. "And we need to get a message to the Resistance."

"I might know someone who can deliver that message," Gabe said. "What is it?"

"Grek is making arrangements to bomb this park in the morning. He thinks the Resistance is underneath it."

"I haven't heard anything about that."

"There is no plan to warn anyone before it happens," Ben said.

Gabe's legs seemed to give way. He caught himself from falling by grabbing the edge of his booth. "I will warn them. I'll also make sure someone warns the vendors in the park."

Gabe closed his booth and spoke to a nearby vendor before heading out of the park. Ben and Selina walked to the people mover and returned to the palace.

24. A New Watcher

Charla was afraid. More afraid than she'd been in her lifetime. Charla had always assumed she could handle anything that came her way, especially since she was a Chosen of the Guardian. But now she was having doubts. Charla assumed all of Grek's powers disappeared when he severed his tie with the Guardian, but it seemed he still retained some. One thing she was sure of was that the Guardian would disapprove of a Watcher using his power to kill.

Charla looked for a place to hide. She wanted somewhere that would limit how much she could grow if she happened to fall asleep. She'd had very little of it in the last thirty-six hours and knew transformations were sometimes lost when a Chosen fell asleep. Finally, Charla found a space between two bricks in the fireplace and climbed in. She didn't fall asleep as she thought she might. Grek was pacing the floor and talking to himself.

"Don't they know I'm the Chosen One? It's their fault if I have to kill them. Kill one and the rest fall into line. Really, I did what I had to, to save lives." He paused and looked around the room. "Who's here with me? I know someone is." Grek walked over to the fireplace and looked up inside the firebox. "Nothing," he muttered. "There's nothing there."

He picked up the poker and slammed it against the hearth. Then he rammed it into the chimney and hit the inside walls of the firebox several times. It struck close to where Charla was hiding just once.

"Where is the there where the something is if the something is not there." He laughed at his own clever speech. "Something, whoever and whatever you are, you'd better just leave. I'm the Chosen One. You can't win against me. You'll only get hurt trying."

Grek walked to the door that led to the pool and disappeared through it. Once he was gone, Charla felt her tense muscles relax. She assumed he was going to touch the Medallion so he could protect his long-lived future. She crawled further into the crack in the brick. Charla leaned back and closed her eyes to rest them. When she opened them again, all the lights were out. Against all expectation, she had been asleep. Charla crawled out of the crack and listened intently. The sound that came back to her was the deep breathing of someone sound asleep. When she looked out the window, she guessed daylight was coming within the hour. If all went according to plan, the Resistance was getting their people in place for an early morning attack on the palace. If ever there was a time to get the Medallion, this was it. She may not have another chance. Charla wondered where Ben was and if he'd warned the Resistance and made it back into the palace. She would certainly feel better if he was here to protect her back. Still, she couldn't wait for him to show up. The time to act was now.

Charla walked over to the door that led to the pool. It was closed. She grew so she could use the door handle, but discovered the door was locked. Grek wasn't taking any chances. She shrunk down and found a tiny crack under the door it might be possible to crawl under if she was small enough. Charla wondered briefly how small was too small. Was there a point at which it became dangerous? What if she couldn't grow again? She wasn't much bigger than the mosquitoes on Ben's world when she was small enough to crawl underneath.

Charla lay flat on her belly and pushed herself underneath the door. Then she stood and grew to her regular size so she could move faster. Charla was going on the assumption that this part of the palace was not monitored. She didn't think Grek would want people watching him day and night. He would want to keep the fact that he was Mer secret. She ran to the pool and threw herself into the water, transforming her legs into a tail. She swam around and around, searching for the entrance to the tube that circled the island. It felt so good to be in water again in her natural form. Charla wanted to take her time and enjoy it, but she swam as fast as she could until she found the opening. On the inside of the tube, she swam around the island several times, getting closer to her goal with each circle. Finally, she came to the end and pulled herself on top of the glass Island. It was now the moment of truth. Would her key fit?

It was hanging around her neck on a chain. She picked it up and lifted it off her head, and fitted it into the lock. It didn't open. Her heart fell, and she was overwhelmed with despair. She'd been through so much, and now the key wasn't going to work. Charla tried again. She tried pushing it in as hard and as far as she could. It still didn't work.

Then she tried pulling it out a little bit before turning it. Her heart rose as the key turned in the lock. She opened the door and took out the Medallion, and decided to carry it out in a way that would leave her hands free. She put it over her head. If Charla had known what would happen next, she would have wrapped the Medallion in something and kept it from touching her. As soon as the Medallion was around her neck, light flared out of it with such brilliance that Charla had to close her eyes. It filled the swimming pool and poured underneath the door. It even found its way into the bedroom of the former Watcher.

Oh no, Charla thought. *The Medallion is making a mistake. It thinks it's in the hands of a new Watcher.* She grabbed for the Medallion to pull it off, but it resisted removal. It didn't feel heavy laying on her chest, but the moment she tried to pick it up, it became so weighty she couldn't move it. It was as if it was a powerful magnet that was attracted to her.

She sat on the ground and rested her head in her hands as images flowed through her mind. Images of former watchers. Images of the world of Mellish and its people. She found herself filled with a deep love for Mellish and a desire to do everything within her power to protect and preserve it. How could Grek have experienced this and be who he is today? She asked herself.

"Beloved child, will you serve me here, or do I search for another?"

She could not have said where the voice came from or whether it was audible, but she knew it was the voice of the Guardian. A deep sense of awe filled her.

There was so much to be lost if she said yes. There were her friends at Fairwaters. There was the lost opportunity to see all of the Six Worlds as a Chosen. There were her parents and her brother. She rarely saw them, but staying here meant she never would. She was silent for some time.

What would happen if she turned the Guardian down? Grief washed over Charla. The surge of grief was almost too much for her to bear. Images flooded her mind of the people suffering, more and more with every year that passed as Grek kept control of the world.

"Yes, I will serve," she whispered. "I will stay and be this world's Watcher." A feeling of deep peace filled her. The peace she felt was not just her own but came from the unseen Guardian who was with her.

The light from the Guardian's Medallion reached Grek's bedroom. It touched his face and then pulled away so quickly that when he opened his eyes, it was gone. He sat up immediately, aware that something significant had changed. He raced out of his bedroom and saw the light coming from underneath the door that led to his swimming area. He ran to the door and tried to open it. He'd forgotten locking the door the night before because of the feeling of not being alone. Obviously, he hadn't been. He ran back to his room, got the key, and brought it back. He also brought with him the key for the vault.

His hands were shaking as he unlocked the door. He threw the key on a nearby table and ran down the hall and into the water. He swam quickly through the tube that circled the place where the Medallion was locked up. He knew as he came out of the water that something had happened, even though nothing appeared changed. He opened the vault door. The Medallion was gone. Rage filled him. He used some of his remaining supernatural power to blast the vault into smithereens and immediately regretted doing so. He had been hoarding his power, knowing that once it was gone, there would be no more.

"You'll be sorry," he screamed out to whoever had his Medallion.

At that point, he did not doubt that he would get it back. He was the Chosen One. The world of Mellish needed him, and he needed the Medallion.

Grek swam back through the pool as a merman then transformed his tail into legs and ran to the outside door. He opened it and spoke to the soldiers standing guard outside. He was completely naked, and the guards stared at him in shock.

"Who has come in and out of my chambers?"

"Just the commanders last night, and the soldiers who came for the body, and Selina."

"Selina?" Grek had never bothered to ask the name of the girl who brought him meals. Could this Selina be involved with whoever took his Medallion? There had to be someone inside the palace helping.

"I want to talk to her. Send word that she is to come up. Also, get the commander back here. I want the soldiers who came and got the body locked up until I get a chance to interrogate them." Grek stared at the soldier and wondered if he could be involved in this conspiracy.

He was in his bedroom and had just put on his pants when he heard the knock. "Just a minute," he called out as he took a clean shirt off its hanger. He was still buttoning the shirt when he opened the door. It was the guard who stood outside.

"The night baker said Selina had a headache and went for a walk. He thinks she should be back any minute."

With those words, Selina rose to the top of the list of those Grek suspected of being disloyal to him.

"I want her brought here the moment she returns, and if she doesn't return within the half-hour, I want troops out looking for her."

"Of course, your excell—"

The soldier's words were cut off by Grek slamming the door.

25. Escape

Mara refused to assign people to attack the palace. It felt like the riskiest assignment of all because it was heavily defended and near the heart of the city. They couldn't return underground after finishing the attack. The only thing they could do was find a place to hide until they could flee from the city. Their chance of getting caught before they could do so was very high.

If the other attack force succeeded in capturing Truehaven, that was where they would go if any of them were able to remain free. Mara laid out the risks and asked if there were any volunteers. There were so many she had to turn people away. Mara was pleased to see that the Dragonborn Chosen, Zane, and Zara, were among those who volunteered for this mission. She thought they might be able to fly away and take some of the Resistance with them when the battle at the palace was lost.

Mara planned to lead the attack herself. She was one of those leaders who would not ask others to do what she herself would not. Mara recognized this might be difficult to survive and felt that she had already lived a long full life. She believed the Resistance could carry on without her as there were many strong leaders in it.

They were still in their underground hideout planning when Gabe arrived with the message that Grek planned to bomb the park. Gabe didn't know exactly when, but he said his father had sent a message from the palace saying it would happen in the morning.

Mara ordered everyone to get their weapons, take whatever personal belongings they valued, and be ready to leave in fifteen minutes. The electronics equipment used by the Resistance had already been packed up and taken to the warehouse. Whatever they couldn't move had been smashed so Grek and his supporters could not retrieve information.

They went through the tunnels to the same warehouse where they had taken the luka beans. Trucks had already started loading supplies. More trunks and drivers waited in an underground parking garage not far from the warehouse, including some they had stolen from the government because they wanted to transport fake prisoners. After each truck was loaded, it left. Those carrying supplies were going to take a slow route to Truehaven so that the ones carrying pretend guards with their prisoners could get there first.

It had taken Ben and Selina longer than anticipated to get back to the palace. The cab driver had not waited for them as he agreed to, even though he'd been paid in advance. They had no choice but to take the people mover, which didn't run as regularly in the middle of the night. When they returned, the guard at the gate leading into the kitchen was the one who had caused so much trouble for

Selina. "Hello sweetheart, I've been waiting for you. Kiss me and I'll tell you why."

"I don't need to know why. Just let me pass."

"Not going to happen. I've waited long enough for that kiss. And you're not going anywhere until I get it."

Selina stepped back and considered her options. This was the only way back to the kitchen, where she was supposed to be working. She didn't want Grek to learn she was missing. What would it hurt to let this guard kiss her? Yet she knew the answer. One kiss would lead to others, and eventually, he would demand more than a kiss. Since Grek had come to power, his soldiers got away with things they would never have gotten away with before. Early in his rule, if the military tried to discipline a rogue soldier, Grek pardoned and promoted them, sending the message that they could do anything as long as they supported him. It was as if he wanted to surround himself with the ruthless and unethical. She'd heard about soldiers extorting people on the street. Complaints about bad behavior fell on deaf ears. Sometimes it was the person who complained who faced punishment. More than one had disappeared, not to be seen again.

Ben was unsure of what to do. He wanted to come to Selina's rescue, but there was so much at stake. Charla was in the palace alone, and he needed to be with her so she could get the Medallion. And yet everything within him raged at what the guard was doing. He struggled to suppress the fire that longed to erupt from within him. He would likely set Selina's coat on fire if it did. He managed to keep the fire down, but he couldn't prevent smoke from escaping his nostrils. The smoke flowed out of Selina's pocket and up her chest as she stepped closer to Geo to give him the kiss he was demanding.

"I don't think I want that kiss, after all," Geo said. "You stink. Have you been smoking ruka bean leaves?" Selina took a sniff and realized there was a smell that hadn't been there before. It never crossed her mind that it could be Ben. She moved to go around Geo, but he grabbed her arm. "Where do you think you're going. I have orders to arrest you."

"You're lying," Selina said.

"You wish," he responded as he tied her hands behind her back. Geo took out a hand radio. "I have her," he said into it.

A few minutes later, two guards came out of the palace and led Selina away with Ben still in her pocket. They were taken directly to Grek. Selina looked at him closely. He seemed to look older than he had when she saw him just a few hours ago. She decided it must be her imagination.

Surely, he wouldn't change that fast even if Charla had succeeded in getting hold of the Medallion.

"Are you a member of the Resistance?" Grek asked Selina.

"Why would you ask me that?"

"I have a traitor in the palace who has helped the Resistance get into my chambers. Is it you?"

"Why would you think I'd do that?"

"Stop answering my question with a question. Is it you?"

"I haven't done anything to be ashamed of."

"What do you mean by that?"

Selina didn't answer his question as fast as Grek wanted. "Never mind. We have ways of making you talk. Put her in a prison cell and call the chief inquisitor." He paused for a moment, then said. "Take her to the cells upstairs rather than the one down here. I want to interrogate this one myself, and the dungeon stinks."

Selina started to speak but didn't know what to say. Her knees felt weak, and her heart was beating rapidly. She'd heard rumors of what the chief inquisitor did. One part of her wanted to yell, "No, please, I'll tell you anything you want to know," the other part wanted to say, "do whatever you want, I'll never talk." Although she knew it wasn't true.

If they tortured her, she would talk. However, she was determined to delay as long as possible to give Ben and Charla a chance to get away. She felt like everything depended on their success. She could bear a little torture, couldn't she?

The guards marched her out the door and took her to the top floor of the palace. There were only three cells on this level. They were usually only used for the prisoners Grek took a particular interest in. All three prison doors were open, the cells empty. Selina was locked in the middle cell. Chains were hanging from a beam in the ceiling. The guards put them around Selina's wrists, and they pulled her arms up over her head, so she had to stand on tiptoes to avoid strain on her shoulders.

After the guard was gone, Ben climbed out of her pocket and jumped toward the floor. As Ben jumped, he grew, hoping he would be big enough not to be hurt by the time he hit the floor. The fall rattled his teeth, but nothing broke.

"What are you doing here?" Selina asked. "You should have tried to get away. You must have known they were taking me to a prison cell."

"Ben has never been very good at making the choice that a wise man would make," a high squeaky voice said. The voice became more normal as Charla grew in size. "But he has always stood by his friends, even if it puts his own life in danger."

"Charla, you shouldn't be here," Ben said.

"How did you get here?" Selina asked.

"I rode up on your foot," Charla said. Then she turned towards Ben, "Like always, we're in this together."

"You have it!" Ben exclaimed when he noticed Charla was wearing the Medallion.

"Yes, I have it, and it has me," Charla said without explaining what she meant.

"What can we do to get Selina out of here?" Ben asked.

"Let's try this," Charla said. "You stand on one side of her, and I'll stand on the other, and we'll see if we can cause Selina to shrink with us as we each hold one of her hands."

"That's not going to work," Ben said.

"Humor me," Charla laughed. "I like that phrase. I learned it on Earth."

"This isn't the time for jokes and laughter," Ben said. "We need a serious plan."

"I am serious," Charla said.

Ben started to object but stopped himself. "You could be right. Besides, we don't have a better plan. Let's give it a try."

Ben took Selina's arm near her right hand close to the chain wrapped around it, and Charla took the other arm.

"Okay, shrink," Charla commanded.

Ben and Charla shrank, and Selina shrank with them. Charla stopped shrinking as soon as Selina's hands were small enough to fall out of the shackles. "Now," she said. "Let's get out of here."

Those words were barely out of her mouth when the Resistance attacked the palace. It was made of stone and built to withstand an attack, but they heard the sound of breaking glass.

"It's time for us to leave," Charla said, and holding the Medallion in her right hand, she reached her left hand toward the door and blew it out of its casing. She reached for Selina's hand and said. "Come on, Ben. We don't have all day."

Ben stood for a moment in shock with his mouth hanging open. He was impressed. Charla had learned how to use the wizard gift exceptionally. He needed to get her to teach him how to do what she did.

A soldier was sitting outside the prison door. He was standing with a look of shock on his face as he scrambled to get out his weapon. He dropped it, picked it up, and pointed it at them. "Stop, now, or I'll shoot."

Charla reached out her hand. The weapon was wrenched out of the guard's hand and flew into hers. Once again, Ben was amazed. He didn't realize having the gifts of a wizard allowed someone to do that. He needed to learn how to control that gift as well as Charla did. Was this why Trevor was so highly valued as a Chosen? Did he have this kind of control over the gift of being a wizard?

They left the guard standing in shock as they walked to the steps leading down. In front of them was the open rotunda. Below them was the pool where Charla had entered the palace for the first time. Above them, there was a dome made of glass. Some of the panels were broken out. The dragons with the Resistance must have dropped an explosive at just that spot. Guards were coming up the stairs from the ground floor.

Ben transformed into a dragon and crouched down. "On my back," he growled in his dragon voice. Charla and Selina did as he asked, and he flew them out of the palace through the broken glass in the dome.

Mara waved to them as they flew overhead. She had ordered Ben to fly directly to Truehaven once he had Charla and the Medallion, and so that is what he did.

26. Truehaven

Dion and Trevor left for Truehaven with six trucks crammed full of some of the best Resistance fighters. A dozen were dressed up in Grek's army uniforms. They had left the city when it was dark and driven with their lights off to a place where they could observe Truehaven as they waited.

The attack on the palace was to start before daylight. They hoped soldiers from the prison would be sent to defend the palace. Dion was beginning to worry that there would be no redeployment when the lights of several vehicles, both ground, and air, could be seen leaving. After the vehicles passed the spot where they were hiding, the Resistance turned on their lights and drove up to the prison gates.

Dion had no choice but to be a prisoner. Her eye scans would be a giveaway if she tried to pass for a guard. So, the guards 'role was being played by Resistance members who had never been arrested and put in prison. Dion had spent a considerable amount of time coaching the supposed guards on what to do and say when questioned. As they drove up to Truehaven, drones came out ready to scan the eyes of anyone who stepped out of the trucks.

Heavily armed guards appeared at the gate. "What's your business here?" one of them asked.

"We have over a hundred escaped prisoners arrested last night to be locked up in your prison," one of the fake guards in the lead vehicle said.

"I haven't heard more prisoners were coming," the guard at the gate said.

"I guess you don't hear everything then."

"And who are you?"

The fake commander gave the name of a less known member of Grek's military guard, so they would find the name on file if they checked. The drones would not raise the alarm because the fake commander had a clean record, and his eyes would not trigger a more in-depth investigation. The guards had handheld scanners, but they usually left the eye scans up to the drones unless they had reason to be suspicious. The drones didn't care if the eyes matched the names; all they were looking for were people whose names had been flagged.

The second guard had gone to look in the back of the trucks. He saw men and women who appeared to be wearing shackles. He watched as the drones gave an alarm, with every person scanned in the back of the truck. Meanwhile, other drones were checking on the eyes of the guards who had accompanied the prisoners. All of the fake guards passed the drone scan.

"It appears that everything is in order, and you are who you say you are," the lead guard said. "I just don't know why we weren't told you were coming. But never mind, the commander will be glad to get these escapees back where they belong."

Truehaven was well fortified. The building was stone, the doors massive. A siege would have taken days, but this way, they drove right into the courtyard when the former school's doors were opened wide to receive them. Some of those returning had been teachers and students here before Grek had gone rogue.

The guards at Truehaven didn't have any real chance of repelling the invaders once they were inside the walls. The fight was almost over before it began. The supposed prisoners threw off the unlocked shackles, picked up the guns hidden behind them, and overwhelmed the guards.

Rather than keep Grek's men in prison where she would need to feed them, Dion took away their boots and clothes and sent them to walk back to the city in their underwear. Not long after, trucks bearing luka beans and other supplies came down the road. The Chosen, who were still in prison cells, were liberated. Most of them needed medical care, and Allison started work, glad for the extra strength the Guardian gave her. She invited Patrice to help her because Allison sensed she could become a healer.

An hour and a half after sunrise, a single dragon appeared in the sky. They watched as it flew directly to them. It landed in the courtyard inside the prison walls, and two women climbed off. The dragon then transformed into Ben.

Dion recognized Charla and guessed the young woman with her must be the one who helped her get in and out of the palace. *Did they have the Medallion, or had they simply decided to leave once the attack started?* She hurried over to Charla. "Did you get it?" she asked.

In answer to her question, Charla pulled the Medallion out from under her t-shirt. Dion put out her hand to take it from Charla, but the Mergirl shook her head and dropped it back under her t-shirt. Dion decided to get it from her later rather than make an issue of it in the courtyard with everyone watching.

The Mer girl seemed to be not quite herself. Perhaps she was in shock. She needed to get the Medallion from Charla at some point and keep it safe until the new Watcher arrived. She was about to reach for it again when Ben stepped between her and Charla.

"This is Selina," Ben said to Dion. "We wouldn't be here if it wasn't for her and her brother's help."

"Thank you so very much," Dion said to Selina as she watched Charla hurry into the former school for the Chosen.

Back in the city, a helicopter was lifting off the ground and heading toward Central Park. The bomb opened a sinkhole in the middle of the city. Friends of Deffon's son had warned people in nearby apartments that construction was happening early in the morning. They were told it was dangerous to remain in their homes. Not everyone left, but most did. The vendors were told the truth. Some of them decided not to be in the park at that time of day, but others believed their leader would not do such a dreadful thing. It was those who were unquestioning in their support of Grek, who died when the bomb dropped.

27. Charla

Mara attacked the palace until the reinforcements from the prison appeared. This was the signal she was waiting for. If their plan was a success, the Resistance had already captured Truehaven. She and a select few continued the battle while the majority of Resistance fighters fled. After providing cover for others to make their escape, Mara and those still fighting with her surrendered. With any luck, Ben and Charla had reached Truehaven with the Medallion. If so, it would be possible for the Guardian to send a new Watcher through a portal if there was no one already on Mellish who was suitable. She had intentionally sent the people she thought might be Watcher material to Truehaven so they could be there when the Medallion arrived.

Chosen did not usually interfere with their own world's politics, but this was an exception to the rule. In this case, a corrupt Watcher was the source of the problem. With the Medallion in the hands of a new Watcher, things would return to normal. Maybe life on Mellish would even become better. With a true Watcher in place, they could work with the Guardian to guide the world to justice and protect the movements that led to peace.

Charla went directly to the residence of the Watcher of Mellish. The memories that continued to flood her mind told her where to find it. The door had been magically locked by Grek when he left to live at the palace, and since then, no one had been able to enter.

Charla touched the door, and it sprang open. She walked over to sit on the Guardian's unique chair. As soon as she did, light erupted from it, flowing through the Medallion into Charla's body before coming out of her eyes, mouth, nose, and ears. She sat in one spot for the next two hours as the power of the Guardian flowed in and through her. After it was over, the light disappeared as abruptly as it had come. When she stood up, she was not the same person.

Charla moved over to the chair behind what was now her desk. Underneath it, she found a footstool for her tail, so she transformed her legs. Charla realized she did not need to transform her human legs into a tail to preserve her strength any longer, but it still felt right and natural to do so. She lay her head back and closed her eyes. Charla felt the presence of the Guardian and heard the words, "Well done, my daughter. There is yet more to do. Know that I am with you and trust in yourself and me." Then she felt the presence of the five other Watchers. She didn't hear their words so much, as have the impression that they were welcoming her as one of them. Then Charla turned her attention to Mellish. The pain of the world caused her to shrink back in her chair. She felt the pain of hungry children. She felt the loneliness of those without family and friends. She experienced the grief of those who had lost a loved one when the park was bombed. She also shared the pride and devotion of parents; the joy when a job is well done—the courage of those who risked their lives for what was right.

Charla touched the fear of the Resistance members who'd been captured and awaited their fate in the palace prison. Among them, she recognized Jared from her homeworld of Lushaka, Mort, and Selina's brother Brent was there. Mara was also in prison, but in a different place in the same building. She touched all those emotions, but she also felt something else. There was a growing sense of hope among those who had fought with the Resistance. For the first time in a long time, some had hope that change was coming.

Hours had passed. Truehaven was firmly under Resistance control. They were waiting for the counter-attack that was sure to come. Dion had noticed Charla was missing at lunch. When she didn't show up at supper sent people out to look for her. If the Mer girl wanted to stay hidden, she might be impossible to find with her ability to shrink and crawl into small places. Dion berated herself for not taking the Medallion out of Charla's hands and putting it somewhere safe until a new Watcher was identified.

When the searchers returned, they hadn't found her. They had even looked in the Pool of Arrival, assuming that a Mer would want to be in the water, but she wasn't there. They had looked high and low, calling out her name so she would know they were looking for her. Dion went to find Ben. He was the only one with them who knew the Mer girl from previous encounters. He might know whether she would intentionally hide and why.

"I'm looking for your friend, Charla," she said. "You know her. Do you have any idea where she could be?"

"No," Ben said. "But did you check the pool?" Dion nodded her head, and Ben continued. "She has always been unpredictable. Don't get me wrong. Charla is brilliant as a Chosen. She is brave and thinks outside the box. She's been responsible for rescuing me more than once. But she's been behaving rather strangely ever since she got the Medallion away from Grek.

"Outside the box? What do you mean?" Dion asked.

"She comes up with new ways of doing what is necessary."

"Do you think she may imagine herself as the next Watcher?"

"With Charla, anything is possible."

"We need to get the Medallion away from her so it can be kept safe."

Ben had a wild thought. What if Charla was the next Watcher? He quickly pushed it away as being highly unlikely. And yet, anything was possible. "Have you looked in the quarters of the Watcher?" he asked.

"No, we didn't look there, the door is locked, and we haven't been able to open it."

"Maybe anyone with the Medallion can get in," Ben said.

"I hadn't thought of that." It crossed Dion's mind that it might help to have someone Charla knew and trusted when she asked her to give back the Medallion. Perhaps the girl had an unhealthy obsession with it. "Let's go check," she said to Ben.

The two of them hurried to the Watcher's home and office. When they pushed on the door, it opened. Charla was sitting at the Watcher's desk. She opened her eyes and smiled at them.

Ben was taken back by the serene look on her face. She seemed to glow with an unnatural light.

"I know what we need to do next," she said as she rose from her chair and came to stand in front of the desk.

"So do I," said Dion as she reached for the Medallion hanging from Charla's neck. Before she could touch it, Charla picked it up and tucked it underneath her shirt.

Doesn't Dion see what I see? Ben thought.

"Charla, you need to give that to me now," Dion said, holding out her hand. "I want to hide it somewhere so we can keep it safe for the next Watcher."

"I am the new Watcher," Charla said.

"Don't be ridiculous," Dion said. "The Guardian wouldn't choose a young Mer girl to be the Watcher on Mellish." She took a step closer to Charla, with her hand reaching toward her neck.

"Dion, wait…" Ben started.

Dion ignored Ben and grabbed for the chain that hung around Charla's neck. She managed to pull the Medallion out from under her shirt. She then reached for it with her other hand. Power erupted from it and threw Dion backward. She sat on the ground, looking up at Charla in shock. Ben reached out and took Dion's hand to help her up. She took a step toward Charla, her legs shaking.

"I guess there's a new Watcher on Mellish," Ben said.

"I guess there is," Dion said before dropping to her knees and bowing her head. "I pledge myself to serve the Guardian of the Six Worlds and the chosen Watcher of Mellish."

Charla took a step forward, so she was standing over Dion. She laid her hands on her head. "Faithful one, long may you continue to serve the Guardian of the Six Worlds.

I promise to do what I can to train you, equip you, protect you, and help you become all the Guardian calls you to be. May you always walk in the light with true companions by your side as you work to restore peace and protect justice on the Six Worlds as one of the Guardian's Chosen."

"Wow, Charla," Ben said. "I never would have dreamed–

–" Ben quit speaking. He didn't know what else to say.

Charla put the Medallion back under her shirt. "Me neither. Not in my wildest dreams. Perhaps it was simply a matter of being in the right place at the right time." A few hours earlier, she would have said, 'the right place at the wrong time. 'Then she turned to Dion. "I have a plan for rescuing the Resistance and the Chosen that Grek has captured. Please send the Dragonborn to me."

There were three Dragonborn Chosen other than Ben. Zane came, as did Zara and Zeke, a dragon who'd been imprisoned with the other Chosen in the special cells Grek had built at Truehaven. Charla sat the Dragonborn on her special chair.

Usually, the chair was only used for the Chosen from Mellish in preparation for going off-world, but Charla felt sure that the Guardian would allow the use she was making of it today. Charla lay her hands on each one of their heads, and they were all given the same gift; the gift of invisibility. They were each given a third gift—the gift of super strength. Two gifts were unusual for shapeshifters. Yet every one of them was given the same two additional gifts in addition to whatever gifts they'd come to Mellish with.

Charla asked that all of the Chosen with the gift of being a wizard meet in the courtyard. There were several. She chose three to come with her on a special mission. One of those selected was Trevor. Not long afterward, they started their flight back to the palace on invisible dragons, which made their riders invisible.

Dion argued that Charla should not go herself, but she insisted she needed to be there to confront Grek in person. He still had some power that belonged to her as the new Watcher. "Besides," she said. "The only one with enough power to defeat a Watcher is another Watcher."

28. On Dragon Wing

When the four invisible Dragonborn and their riders flew over the outskirts of Nortown, they saw a line of armored trucks heading toward Truehaven. It included not only the soldiers previously stationed there but additional soldiers for the upcoming battle.

Ben circled Central Park so everyone could see the damage. A large cavern had opened in the ground where the park had been. The nearby apartment buildings were flattened. Buildings further away had parts of their walls missing. The lucky ones just had windows blown out. Bricks and glass littered the ground for blocks around.

When they arrived at the palace, they noticed scaffolding erected to repair the dome's broken glass. The heavy plate glass windows were still broken, which made entering easy for those who could fly. They dropped into the palace and made a circle in the rotunda above the pond until they were in line with the top of the stairs on the fourth floor.

There were no guards outside the prison doors, which surprised Charla. It made her doubt the impression she'd had of prisoners held here. Perhaps they'd been moved since she'd sat in her office and sent that part of her that was a Watcher out into the world.

When they landed, they were surprised to see that the room where they had blown the door off its hinges was not empty. Mort was standing in the center of the room. Nothing seemed to be holding him in place, but he stood unmoving on what looked like a brick.

"It's a bomb," he whispered. "The moment I step off, it will explode. I've been standing here for hours. You'd better get out of here because I don't know how much longer I can keep this up."

Charla saw that Mort's legs were shaking, and there was a sheen of sweat on his face.

"What can we do?" Zara whispered.

"I know what to do," Trevor said. "I'll pick the brick up with Mort on it and carry it to the balcony. As I drop it, one of the Dragonborn needs to simultaneously snatch Mort and hopefully fly fast enough to get him away from the explosion. Does anyone have a better idea that is less dangerous?"

No one responded.

"You are super strong, but a bomb can still injure you. I wish I could think of another solution." Charla paused. "Are you sure you want to do this?"

Trevor nodded.

"Are one of the Dragonborn willing to take the risk?" Charla asked. She could tell that Zara was about to volunteer. As Charla looked at Zara, scars appeared on her face. She knew Zara would end up badly injured if she were the one to do this. Charla turned away from Zara and looked at Ben. Before that moment, she hadn't known that part of a Watcher's gift was the ability to discern what would happen in the future if specific actions were taken.

"I'll do it," Ben said.

Trevor crouched down with his legs spread apart and his back straight and put a hand on each side of the brick. Once he had a good hold, he slowly straightened his knees until he was upright. Mort wavered just a bit, and it looked like he was about to lose his balance. But then he caught himself by placing his hand on Trevor's head. Trevor took one careful, slow step after another until he was standing beside the balcony rail. Ben walked with him in his human form. Trevor lifted the brick with Mort on it over the rail.

"Are you ready?" Trevor asked Ben.

Ben nodded and moved over to the stairs, where he transformed and leapt into the air. A few seconds later, as Ben started to lift Mort into the air, Trevor let go of the brick. He threw himself away from the bomb as it exploded. Ben held Mort in his arms and spun around so his back would be toward the bomb. He flung himself upward, holding Mort close to his belly to try to protect him from the blast. The force of the explosion pushed Ben upward through the already broken pane of glass. Panes that hadn't previously broken now shattered and rained down into the pond.

Ben looped around above the palace and flew back inside to drop Mort down beside Trevor, who was rolling on the ground, trying to put out the fire burning the bottom of his pant legs. Ben used his wing to smother it. Mort helped Trevor take his still too hot pants off. His calves were red and starting to blister.

It crossed Ben's mind that if Trevor didn't return, he'd have a chance with Allison, but he pushed the idea away, horrified he had thought it. At that moment, Ben knew he would do everything he could to get Trevor back to Allison alive.

"Are you okay?" Ben asked Trevor.

"It hurts," Trevor said.

"Allison will make it better," Ben said.

Charla came and crouched down beside Trevor and put her hands on his head. As Ben watched, the blisters disappeared and the redness faded. "You'll need to put your pants back on," she said. "We've got people to rescue."

Ben was amazed. No one had told him a Watcher could heal. Maybe not all of them could.

The bomb had warned the soldiers that a rescue was underway, and they were slowly coming up the stairs. Ben,

Charla, and the others went into the cell and stood against the wall with their invisibility turned on.

"There's no one here," the lead soldier reported as he looked into the room where Mort and the brick had been.

"But how did the bomb get moved, so it exploded in the rotunda, and where is the prisoner?" the soldier behind him asked.

"I don't know, but there's no one here now."

"Is it possible they got into the other cells?"

"How could they? They're all booby-trapped. If they had tried to open the doors, the bombs would have exploded, and we would be picking up body parts."

"Maybe if we leave, they'll come back and try to open one of the doors." The soldiers turned and walked back down the stairs.

"The doors are booby-trapped," Charla said once they were gone. 'Somehow, I missed that."

"I guess that's why they have no guards," Ben said.

"We should have guessed when we saw Mort that there would also be a problem with the doors," Trevor said.

"It's a good thing we can go through walls if we need to," Charla said. "I want a Dragonborn and two wizards on each wall. The dragons will blast with fire while the wizards hit them with an electric charge. Target the mortar. Be as quiet as you can. I will also do what I can to dampen the sound with my abilities as a Watcher. Once we make a small hole, then those with super strength can pull the bricks out and make it large enough for a human to go through."

"Let's put the door back in place. It's thick and will keep most of the sound inside the room," Trevor said.

Ben and Zara focused dragonfire on a brick near the bottom of the wall. Trevor and another Chosen from Earth named Scott sent electrical charges ramming into the same spot. Chunks of mortar and shards of brick flew out and landed on the floor. On the other side of the room, the same thing was happening. Trevor bent down and felt the brick. It was too hot to touch with his hands. He laid down on his back, brought his legs up toward his chest, and then kicked at the wall. An ordinary person likely would not have been able to make a difference, but with a kick from a Chosen gifted with super strength, the brick broke off and flew into the cell on the other side of the wall.

"Wait," Ben said. "Let me go through to the other side and make sure everything is okay, and we're not putting the people in there in danger."

Ben shrunk down in size and crawled through the hole. On the other side, he grew.

Shouts of 'thank you Guardian 'and 'praise God 'rang out from the people in the room when they saw who it was. There were seven prisoners—five men and two women were chained to the wall directly opposite the door. Some were wounded. One person hung unconscious from the wall, blood dripping from their wounds. Instruments used for torture hung on the wall across from the one they were breaking through.

Ben started to speak, but Trevor spoke over his voice. "Well, is it okay for us to keep working?"

"There's no one in danger of being hurt by flying bricks," Ben said.

"Okay then, get back here so we can make a hole big enough for the prisoners," Trevor ordered.

The tone of his voice made Ben's dragonfire flare. Did Trevor think he was too dumb to know he should do that without being told?

"Hurry and get us out of here," one of the chained prisoners called out as Ben crawled back through the hole.

They once more attacked the wall with fireballs and dragon fire. This time Scott used his legs as a jackhammer and broke away the weakened bricks. They repeated this procedure until they had a hole large enough for an adult.

Trevor and Scott went to the prisoners, each grabbing a piece of chain to try to yank it out of the wall. Ben stopped them.

"Let's be smart about this." Ben took the key down from where it hung on a hook by the door and used it to open the cuffs holding the prisoners to the chain. One of the people rescued was Jared.

When the prisoners were in the central cell, Charla noticed that Jupe, Mara, and Brent were missing. There may have been others, but she asked about those three because she knew them.

"Jupe is dead, but the other two were alive the last we saw them," a Resistance fighter Charla hadn't yet met said. "Once they brought us into the palace, they scanned our eyes and took those two away."

Charla was silent for a moment. "I think I know where they are. They are on the same level as Grek lives on." She paused for a few seconds, then spoke again. "This is what we are going to do. Three Dragonborn are going to take those we've already rescued back to Truehaven right away. One of the Dragonborn will stay with me. I would also like to have one other stay."

"I'll stay," Jared said quickly.

"Not this time, my friend," Charla smiled at Jared fondly.

"I'll stay," Trevor said.

"Me too," Scott added.

Charla smiled at Scott. "Scott, I think you should go back to Truehaven and join the fight there. Ben and Trevor will come with me. Everyone, please be as quiet as you can once we leave this prison cell. My sound dampening magic is only working in this room."

Moments later, three dragons took off with their passengers and flew through the dome's broken glass, unseen by those standing below. The passengers who did not have the gift of invisibility became so once they were on the dragon's backs.

When Charla looked over the railing, she noticed several men and women standing guard on each of the levels below them. They were looking out over the balcony rails. There were several more on the ground level who were looking up into the rotunda. The top stair on each landing had a barrier in front of it. No one could continue down the stairs from one floor to another without moving the obstacles that were the same height as the banisters.

The soldiers had turned off light lines that went back and forth across the open space above the pool and the surrounding lobby. It was a tactical error that Charla and her company could take advantage of. If it were functioning, it would have alarmed several times with dragons' flight whether they were visible or invisible.

"It would be helpful if we could get those guards to come up here," Ben said.

"Well, we could try blowing one of the doors off its hinges," Trevor suggested.

"Do it," Charla said. "But do it from Ben's back."

"Good plan," Trevor said. "Let's see if the doors are actually booby-trapped."

Ben transformed into a dragon, and the other two climbed on. He hovered just above the banister as Trevor released fireballs at the door hinges from his invisible hands. There was no explosion after several direct hits, so he targeted the handle. Finally, there was a blast that sent Ben and his passengers flying backward through the air. The fire touched Ben's belly but did no significant damage to him or his riders.

Guards ran up the stairs as Ben silently drifted down to the ground level. He gently moved his wings to keep the sound to a minimum as he flew over the heads of the guards who remained standing around the pool. One of the guards looked up and around, but he kept quiet about the unexpected breeze when he didn't see anything. Ben landed behind him in the hallway that led to the kitchen. The two people on his back got off, and he transformed back into a human. The three of them held hands as they walked toward the elevator.

There were likely stairs somewhere leading down to the basement, but Ben didn't know where to find them. He didn't think opening one door after another to look for them would be a good idea. A female guard was walking back and forth in front of the elevator. The three companions pressed themselves against the wall on their left as she walked by. At the elevator, they waited until she was just about at the end of her cycle to push the button. Unfortunately, it was in the basement when they called it up, and the doors didn't open until the guard was passing directly in front of it. She stepped into the elevator and, finding nothing there, stepped back out, and kept walking. The door closed behind her. This time Ben waited until the guard passed the elevator again before pushing the button. The door opened, the guard turned around but seeing nothing, she kept walking. The companions hurried through the door, and Ben pushed the button, which would take them down to the basement.

29. The Dungeon

When the elevator door opened, Charla led the way.
Instead of going right towards Grek's residence, she led
them left to the heavy metal door guarded by a soldier.
They walked straight toward him, cloaked in invisibility.
They were wondering how they were going to get through
the door when they heard voices behind them. Charla
recognized one of the voices. It was Grek.

The other voice was one she didn't know. She listened to
it as it came closer. "The only thing we've been able to get
out of the woman were things we already knew. She
affirmed that she was the Resistance leader. She told us
they were living under the city and have now moved to
Truehaven. We haven't been able to get her to betray her
contacts or tell us if they had people working for them here
at the palace or the Truehaven prison. She claimed the
serving girl wasn't working for them."

"Liar," Grek snarled. "Have you got anything from her
brother?"

"He keeps saying she wasn't part of the Resistance. So
far, he hasn't broken under torture."

"Pick up their parents," Grek instructed. "We'll see what
he has to say when we tear his mother's fingernails off."

"Shrink," Charla whispered before the two men reached the door. They shrunk and moved into the corner where the hall met the wall the door was in. Grek stopped and stared into that corner. He grabbed the weapon from the guard standing by the door and sprayed the walls in the corner with a blast intended to kill. He went back and forth across the two walls, going lower with each pass until both walls were pockmarked. Meanwhile, the invisible companions, about the size of small mice, were on their knees with their arms over their heads. They were as close to the wall as they could get, each one struggling not to cry out in pain as fragments of rock rained down on them.

When the blasts stopped, Charla turned around and looked at Grek. He looked older than he did the day before. His hair was thinner, and his skin more wrinkled. It appeared that he had lost a tooth sometime during the night.

The two soldiers standing nearby were trying to mask the alarm they felt at such bizarre behavior. Their eyes were wide, and there were worry lines across their foreheads as they stared at Grek.

"Don't look at me like that," he growled. "I know what I'm doing."

"We haven't been able to get the Resistance leader to talk about what their plans are," the soldier who had walked down the hallway with Grek said, his voice strained.

"That's because they have none," Grek snarled. "Their only plan is to make my life as miserable as possible."

"I'm sure you're right, your Excellency." The soldier quickly turned to the soldier guarding the door. "What are you waiting for? Open up."

When the door was open, Grek and the soldier accompanying him walked through. Charla and those with her quickly ran through the door before it was closed again.

The companions found themselves in a long dark hallway that smelled of puke and stale pee, and other unidentifiable odors. The smell was enough to make Ben choke. It tickled his throat, and he had to work hard to suppress a cough. His eyes started to water almost immediately. He didn't know if it was a reaction to the stench or from the deep sadness he felt for anyone imprisoned in this place. Whatever it took, he wanted to get everyone who was in this prison out of it.

Ahead of them, they heard moans. They passed a dark cell and knew someone was inside it because they were crying.

"We will open this door later," Charla said. "First, we must take care of Grek."

Ahead of them, a dim light was shining through an open prison door.

"So, this is the serving girl's brother," they heard Grek say. "And you tell me he failed to show up to serve in my army when conscripted."

"That's right, your Excellency," the soldier who had escorted him into the prison said.

"And has he any excuse?" Grek asked.

"None, whatsoever," said the nasal voice of a third person. "In fact, he confessed to being a Resistance sympathizer."

"He didn't confess to being part of the Resistance?" Grek asked.

"No, but that doesn't mean he wasn't," the nasal voice said. "He could be just trying to protect his friends."

"How about his sister?" Grek asked.

"He keeps insisting his sister is not and never has been a Resistance member."

"That's a lie! I know it is," Grek snarled.

By then, the companions had reached the door, still shrunken in size, they looked into the cell from near the floor.

Brent took a deep, shuddering breath. "Sister... not in Resistance. I know nothing." It was hard to understand what he was saying as he croaked out the words.

"We'll see how much you know when we torture your parents," Grek said. "I'm ordering their arrest, but I thought I'd give you a chance to tell the truth first."

"Pleeease…No," Brent cried out. "I'm telling you the truth. I don't know anything."

Charla grew in size, and the other two followed her. She gestured that they were to remain hidden behind the door. "He's telling the truth," she said, causing the men in the room to turn around in shock. The two guards leveled their weapons at her while the torturer who owned the nasal voice picked up a long stick with a trigger on one end. Charla assumed he used it to shock prisoners.

"Who are you?" Grek asked. "What are you doing here?"

"My name's Charla, and I'm here to rescue your prisoners, of course."

"I knew there was someone there. You must be a Chosen with the gift of invisibility. You did well to avoid my attack. But you're no match against the power of a Watcher."

"You are no longer a Watcher," Charla said.

"Perhaps not, but I still have powers that are greater than any Chosen?"

"Your powers are diminishing every day."

"You think so, do you?"

"I know so because you've lost the Medallion."

"I didn't lose it; it was stolen. I imagine you took it. Give it back. It belongs to me."

"It's not your Medallion anymore."

"If you give it back to me, I'll let these people live."

"I'm not stupid enough to believe that."

"Okay, give it back to me, and you'll have a quick death rather than a painfully slow one at the hands of this man." Grek gestured to the man standing on the other side of Brent with the nasal voice. "He doesn't look like much," Grek continued. "but he's very good at his job."

The torturer leered at Charla. "It would be my pleasure to give you pain like you've never imagined possible."

"Hm," Charla said as if considering that option. "I don't think so. I've become rather attached to this trinket." She pulled the Medallion out from underneath her shirt and held it in her hand.

Grek stepped forward, then stopped, and turned to the soldier who had been in the room with the inquisitor before anyone else arrived. "Go get the Medallion from her."

Ben and Trevor stepped out from behind the door frame. "I don't think so," Ben said, sending a blast of energy at the guard nearest to him, knocking the weapon out of his hands. Trevor did the same thing to the other guard. They howled in pain as they both cradled their wounded hands. The torturer lowered his weapon and waited for further instructions from Grek. The former Watcher raised his hands to blast them with whatever energy he still possessed. Charla ignored Ben and Trevor's protests and stepped in front of them, holding the Medallion in front of her toward Grek. As she guessed, he did not want to risk damaging it. She moved toward Grek so that he was only one step away from being able to grab the Medallion. He reached out for it, but Charla grabbed his arm. Grek started to jerk as if touched by a wire full of electric current.

"Who are you?" Grek screamed as a blue light flashed out of the Medallion and struck him in the chest.

"I'm the new Watcher, which means you can't take the Medallion from me. I have to give it to you, which will never happen willingly."

"Let go of me," Grek whimpered, trying to yank his arm out of her grasp.

"I'm sorry, but you have power that belongs to me." Sparks danced around Charla's hand as she held Grek's arm.

When she was satisfied, Charla let Grek go, and he fell to his knees. The aging process had sped up. Hair that had fallen from his head lay on his jacket and the floor around him. Also, on the floor were two more teeth. His back bent, and his body shriveled. As they watched, his hands turned grey, and pieces broke away. He wasted away until all that was left was a pile of clothing mixed with ash.

Meanwhile, Trevor took the guard's weapons from them, broke them in two, and threw them into the left corner near the door. Ben freed Brent and was helping him out of the prison cell. Charla followed them out, and they locked the two guards and the torturer inside.

They checked all the other cells. Mara was in the cell where they had heard someone crying. They also found a man who was barely alive in a third cell. The man was filthy and he stank. His grey hair was long and thin. What clothing he still possessed hung loosely on his body. He stared at them in terror, striking out when they came close. Trevor took hold of the older man's arms and he cried out in pain. So, Trevor gently lifted him from the floor to carry him out, cradled in his arms.

They retraced their steps to the door guarded by one of Grek's soldiers. "Open the door," Trevor demanded. They quickly disarmed the guard. The soldier standing in front of the door leading into Grek's residence shot at them. Ben sent a lightning bolt, which hit him square in the chest. He was wounded but still alive. He dropped his weapon and put his hands over his head as far as the pain allowed him to.

The older man, by now, was more aware of what was happening. "You're rescuing me," he whispered.

"That's right," Trevor said as he once more cradled the man in his arms.

Tears started to flow down the old man's cheeks. "I lost hope," he whispered.

They took the elevator to the main floor, and Charla led them to the kitchen. The daytime serving woman screamed in terror as they walked through the door. The day cook picked up a large butcher knife but quickly put it down and backed away from it with his hands up. Charla went to the door and opened it. At the gate leading out of the little courtyard was the guard who had given Selina so much trouble. Ben was already transforming into a dragon when he leveled his weapon and pulled the trigger. The charge hit Ben, the dragon, in the chest and did absolutely no damage. Ben breathed dragonfire, and the guard fell to the ground in flames.

Ben, the dragon, knelt so the others could climb on. They placed the unknown man in front of Trevor, who put his arm around him to keep him from falling. Brent was behind Trevor, followed by Mara, who was in better shape than the others. Charla climbed on behind her. The gift of super-strength meant Ben could easily carry them all.

Ben took a short run and leapt into the air, rising as quickly as he dared. They soared up and over the palace, avoiding the square where several of Grek's soldiers stood guard. The soldiers guarding the back of the palace were taken by surprise. The few shots they managed to get off before Ben was out of range missed their target. After those first shots, Ben remembered he could become invisible, and everyone on his back would be invisible as well.

30. Felix Amerge

When Ben and the others arrived back at Truehaven, Grek's soldiers were outside the walls. Ben was glad for the gift of invisibility as he soared over their heads to land on the other side of the wall. As soon as they were visible, Selina came running out of the shadows. Others also came to help the wounded off of Ben's back.

"Where's Allison?" Charla asked. "We have some seriously wounded people that need her."

"She's with the Chosen we freed when we got here," a short, plump woman said. "I'll go get her."

Selina and a teenage boy standing nearby helped Brent walk through the front door of Truehaven into the large foyer. They sat him down on a nearby bench. Others helped Mara walk in. The other man they'd rescued was carried in and laid on the floor in front of the seat Brent sat on.

It didn't take long for Allison to arrive. She immediately sank to the ground beside the skeletal man and sent her healing spirit into him to assess the damage. "It's a wonder this man is still alive," she said. "There are many broken bones. Some were broken a long time ago. Others are more recent. The nerves in his hands are damaged, some beyond repair. His body is severely malnourished. I can't do anything about that last problem. It will take time and good food to restore him to full health."

Allison kept the rest of her thoughts to herself. This man was never going to be the man he was before imprisonment. She couldn't fix all the damage done months before. The other thing Allison couldn't fix was the missing teeth. Some were broken by the abuse he experienced. Others had fallen out due to not having an adequate diet for a long period of time. What she did do was extract the roots of the broken teeth. She couldn't imagine the pain this man had experienced and was still experiencing. She repaired the damage to his kidneys and then started healing one broken bone after another.

"Who is it?" more than one voice asked.

"I think it could be Felix," someone said hesitantly.

"His hair is black, and this man's hair is white," someone objected.

"Felix also weighs about ten times as much as this man," another person said.

"Still," a new voice said. "There is something about him that reminds me of the former Prime Minister. The bone structure and height are the same. And the nose. Noses don't change when someone loses weight."

"When Grek took over, he claimed the Prime Minister was dead and that before he died, he appointed him to head the government."

"It's possible he lied."

"More than possible. I'd die of shock if that man ever told the truth."

The man Allison was healing groaned and took hold of her arm. "Where am I?" he croaked.

"We've rescued you," Allison said. "You're here at Truehaven with the Resistance."

The man burst into fresh tears.

Dion fell to her knees beside Allison. "Who are you," she asked.

"Felix Amerge," he barely whispered the words, which caused a great stir among those gathered at the door. Then he spoke louder. "I am Felix Amerge, the Prime Minister of Mellish, elected to serve by the goodwill of the people. Grek had—" which was as far as he got before he burst into tears again.

Allison patted his shoulder before standing up so she could heal Mara and Brent.

"What's been happening here?" Charla asked Dion.

"The soldiers outside our walls seem to be waiting for instructions," Dion said. "So far, they have neither attacked nor issued any demands."

Charla turned and started to walk away. Then she stopped and stood where she was with her eyes closed. "I need a couple of Dragonborn with riders who have the wizard gift to check out the mountain behind Truehaven," she said when she opened her eyes. "Make it look like you are flying away, but then circle around and come over the mountain from behind. Keep watch from up there until the battle starts or until it is dark."

"I'll go," Ben said.

"You need to know that the gift of invisibility ended the moment you landed back in Truehaven. The only gifts you still have are the ones given on your own world," Charla said.

"Would you be willing to have me as your rider?" Trevor asked Ben.

There was an uncomfortable silence until Ben nodded. "I'll meet you back here in fifteen minutes," he said.

"Great," Trevor answered. "I'll grab something to eat and be ready when you are."

"I'll go," Zane said.

"I'll go with Zane if he'll take me," A tall woman with black hair named Bethany said. Bethany had graduated from Fairhaven a few years before Ben became a student there.

"My pleasure," Zane responded.

Trevor was waiting outside the door in the courtyard when Ben arrived. As Trevor was climbing on his back, Ben realized that he trusted Trevor to do what was right even though they didn't get along. Trevor would do everything he could to make sure this mission was a success, and they both came back in one piece. Ben knew at that moment that he would do the same for Trevor. There were some things more important than personal disagreements.

Ben and Zane rose into the air and flew to the right away from the soldiers outside the gates. They flew around to the mountain's backside and then up past the tree line and over the top. The air temperature dropped the higher they went. It didn't bother Ben, but he wondered how Trevor was doing. He landed on a ledge that gave them a good view of the school. Zane found a ledge of his own off to the right. Ben saw a white line below him and wondered what it was. When he looked closer, he realized it was a rope and assumed the Chosen used it for training purposes. Like the students at Fairhaven, the students at this school would learn to rappel. He was looking for other ropes when he heard a weapon discharge at the front of the school. A few seconds later, a gun discharged directly below him on the mountain. He'd been wrong about the rope. It hadn't been left there by students from Truehaven; Grek's soldiers had recently placed it there. He was well hidden, but Ben saw where the blast from his weapon originated. He shot again and hit the back of the school, cracking the rock wall.

The school had no way to defend itself when an attack was launched from the mountain. The builders had never envisioned a day when an attack would come from that direction. Actually, Ben doubted they'd ever anticipated a day when they would be under attack from any direction.

Ben, Zane, and their riders were the only ones who could prevent the mountain attackers from doing significant damage. They rose silently into the air and hung there for a moment as they scanned for weapon's fire. They needed to take care not to make themselves easy targets for shooters they couldn't see. They didn't move until guns fired from four different places on the mountain; Ben dove toward the nearest one. When he got close enough, he let out a big blast of dragon fire while Trevor hit the same spot with a bolt of energy. A weapon clattered down the mountain as it fell. When they flew closer, they caught sight of the soldier who had fired it. He wore clothing that enabled him to fit into his surroundings and had covered himself with branches that he had cut from nearby trees. He had suffered a direct hit and wasn't moving. Zane and Jared had taken out a second soldier. There were two more left. The soldiers were no longer targeting Truehaven but had turned their weapons on Ben, Zane, and their riders.

"There," Trevor said, pointing out a flash of light.

Ben dodged the missile without seeing its source. "Where?"

"To your right, near the big tree stump," Trevor said.

Ben flew closer. The missiles had a better range than either dragon fire or the wizard gifts. He and Trevor targeted the right of the stump a second before the soldier fired. The missile hit just behind where Trevor was sitting on Ben's back and was deflected away by the scales that covered Ben's body. He banked to the right and flew by the tree stump. Trevor sent a ball of fire at the soldier, and they heard panicked cries of pain. Ben targeted the spot with dragon fire and there was silence.

Ben looked for his next target. Zane was flying directly at a spot on the mountain with dragon fire blazing. Bethany was leaning out, trying to get a good angle of attack. A flash of light exploded in front of them and tore off one of Zane's wings. He flapped the remaining wing and crashed into the spot where the missile had come from. Bethany jumped from his back while Zane hit the mountainside and tumbled toward the ground, where he lay unmoving. Ben roared his rage and grief at the sight of Zane lying broken on the ground below him.

Bethany was struggling with the soldier who had just killed Zane. He was heavier than she was, but she had been trained in the Marshall Arts and had moves the soldier did not expect. Their battle ended when Bethany flipped the soldier over her back, and he tumbled down the mountainside to lie in a crumpled heap.

Ben was flying toward Bethany to see if there was enough room to land and pick her up when a weapon opened fire on him. There were not four soldiers, but five. One had not revealed him or herself until now. The missile hit the tip of Ben's wing and deepened the rage he felt. His anger was so intense it pushed out every rational thought. Part of his brain knew that the season of Wrathborn was preventing him from thinking clearly. He had managed to keep it under control for the last few days, but now the pain, the fear, and the grief caused it to erupt and drive out every other thought but the need for revenge.

He turned to where he had seen the weapon fire and flew directly at it. He didn't take even a second to think of a strategic move or about the passenger on his back, but he flew straight at the soldier. The weapon fired again, and the missile hit him square in the chest. Usually, his dragon scales offered protection. But he was too close, and the weapon was powerful. It punched right through his scales and pierced his chest. Ben crash-landed on top of the man who had shot him, sending Trevor flying through the air to hit the mountainside. All three of them lay unmoving.

31. Allison

Allison knew the moment it happened that something had gone terribly wrong, and Trevor and Ben needed her.

"Do what you can," she said to Patrice, who could now heal simple things on her own.

"Where are you going?" Wounded patients cried out as she walked away without explanation. She knew Ben and Trevor would die if she didn't get to them quickly.

Allison went to the courtyard and scanned the area for Zara. She figured the Dragonborn girl would be in the thick of the battle and she was right. Zara was standing on the wall in her human form, sending fireballs down at the army that surrounded Truehaven. She too had the gift of wizarding.

"Zara," Allison cried out from below the place where Zara stood. "I need you. Ben and Trevor are in trouble."

Zara turned away from the battle and stared down at Allison. "How do you know that?"

"I just do. I've had it happen before. It's not uncommon for some healers to just know things."

"What do you want me to do?"

"They are somewhere on the mountain behind us. Carry me up there so I can look for them."

Zara nodded her head and took the wooden stairs down from the walkway at the top of the wall. "Do we need to go right away?" she asked Allison when she got close to her.

Allison swallowed back the tears that were threatening to engulf her. "Yes, I feel it is a matter of life and death."

Zara transformed into a dragon and crouched down so Allison could climb on her back. They didn't fly around the backside of the mountain like Ben and Zane had. Instead, they flew straight up the mountain from the school. They hadn't gone far when Zara noticed the broken body of Zane lying on the ground. He was near the mountain outside the wall that surrounded the school on three sides. Some of Grek's soldiers were attempting to break scales free from his body. They had a knife out and were hacking away. Zara dove toward them without making a sound. When she got close enough to do some real damage, she sent a torrent of dragonfire in their direction. The three soldiers burst into flame, dropped to the ground, and rolled to try to put themselves out.

Zara landed beside Zane, and Allison slid off her back and placed her hand on his head. She closed her eyes for a moment, and when she opened them, shook her head. Zara roared and spewed fire. Allison avoided the fire as she hurried back to Zara and climbed on her back. Zara was inclined to stay and defend Zane's body, but Allison finally got her back into the air. They zigzagged across the mountain, looking for signs of Ben and Trevor. They caught sight of Bethany and Ben at the same time. Bethany was waving to attract their attention, while Ben's back legs and tail were hanging down from the ledge he'd landed on.

"We'll be back for you later," Allison yelled at Bethany as they flew past her to where Ben and Trevor were.

"I can't land there," Zara said. "But there's a spot above them where it's possible to land. There's a rope. We can rappel down."

"No, I can't do that," Allison said. "Are you sure you can't land where they are?"

"I'm sure. Ben is filling up the spot where it might have been possible. If I try to land, I'm likely to send him tumbling down the side of the mountain."

Allison did not reply. Zara took it as confirmation they were going to do as she suggested and so landed on the ledge where the top of the rope was.

Allison thought back on her time inside the mountain when she had to rappel down the chimney cave. She'd been terrified to begin her descent even though she was wearing a harness and in no real danger. Here, she would be in danger. There was no harness. When her class had rappelled down a cliff near Fairhaven, she had watched but managed to find an excuse that kept her from doing it herself. Now, she wished she hadn't avoided practicing with her class.

Looking down the cliff, she could see Trevor's crumpled body. She couldn't tell if he was breathing or not. She needed to get down there, and she had no time to waste.

Allison was shaking as she stepped inside the parallel ropes. There was only one long rope, the ends of which hung down in parallel tracks down the side of the mountain. The first thing she had to do was check and make sure the ropes were the same length. She stood between the two ends and picked up one end in each hand. She stepped inside the rope, which she then wrapped around her waist and pulled between her legs. She then brought the two pieces of rope from behind her back and held them together in her right hand. She picked up the rope in front of her with her left hand so that each hand held the rope and the rope itself made a harness.

Her hands were shaking as she backed up toward where the mountain fell away. She stood balanced on the very edge, unsure as to whether she really could do this. If she fell, it would kill her, and that would do no one any good. But she had to try because the lives of her friends depended on it. She closed her eyes and took several deep breaths. Then she bent her knees and stepped off the cliff. She wanted to keep her body as close to the mountainside as possible but knew she had to lean her upper body away from it as she walked down with her feet.

It didn't take long before she had a rope burn on both her hands. And the rope between her legs was distinctly uncomfortable. However, the only thing she could do was keep going, letting a little bit of rope out at a time as she moved down the face of the cliff. Her whole body was shaking when she stepped out of the rope on the ledge where Trevor and Ben were.

She dropped down beside Trevor. He was severely hurt. She sent enough healing power into him to keep him alive and then went to check on Ben. His left lung was punctured, and his heart was traumatized by the missile that had broken through his scales. His heartbeat was erratic, and his breath was rapid and shallow. His eyes were glazed over, and she knew he didn't have long to live.

She pulled the missile out and acted quickly to stop the blood that came gushing out with it. She sent her healing power into Ben and healed the puncture in his lung and his heart enough to keep him from dying immediately. She started closing the hole in his chest but stopped short of completely healing it. She then checked the man whose arm was sticking out from underneath Ben and discovered he was dead. That was a relief. She did not need to agonize about whether to heal this enemy soldier or not.

For a moment, she was uncertain who to heal first and then decided it would take more of her energy to finish healing Ben in his dragon form than it would take to heal Trevor. She moved over to Trevor and placed her hands on his body. Several vertebrae were crushed, and he had a concussion from hitting the mountain head first. Brain injuries were tricky things to heal, but she slowed her breathing and sent her spirit as a healer into his body. When she finished, he was lying on the ground, groaning, still in some pain from the trauma he'd experienced. If Ben did not require healing, she would have healed every part of Trevor that was causing pain, but Ben needed her more than Trevor needed to be pain-free.

By the time she returned to Ben, Zara had come down the rope as a human and was crouched out of the way watching her. Allison used her gift as a healer to finish stabilizing Ben's heart, and then she finished closing the wound in his chest. She could not restore the broken scales. Only time itself could do that. She knew her power was working when Ben transitioned from a dragon into a human. He rolled off the dead man onto his back, touched his chest, and said, "Ouch."

By this time, Trevor was sitting up, with his head in his hands, groaning. Allison moved back over to Trevor and put her hand on top of his head, and took away most of the pain he was experiencing.

Ben was sitting up, silently staring out into space. He was ashamed of himself. He had not only put himself and Trevor in danger, but he had put Allison in danger as well. And there were people in the battle below that were not being healed because the healer was here with them. He didn't hear Allison when she spoke to him the first time.

She had to repeat herself. "Can you transition back into a

dragon and fly back to the school?" She asked for a second time.

"Of course," Ben said.

He stood, transitioned, and leapt off the side of the mountain. Flight was painful but certainly possible.

He noticed Bethany as he flew beside the mountain. He perched beside her long enough for her to climb onto his back. Then he quickly dropped down to the courtyard where Zara had already landed with Allison and Trevor.

As soon as she landed, Allison slipped off Zara's back and ran into the school turned into a prison. The wounded from the on-going battle were just inside the door waiting for her.

Ben transitioned from dragon to human. Trevor was starting to walk away when Ben called his name. "Trevor," he said.

Trevor turned and looked at him, his eyes wary. "Yes."

"I just want to say—" Ben stopped and stared at his feet.

"Yes."

"I just want to say—I'm sorry. I came close to killing both of us."

Trevor took a step back toward Ben, reached out his hand, and squeezed his shoulder without saying a word. Then he turned and walked away, leaving Ben to his own thoughts.

32. General Gillenbran

Ben followed Trevor to the command center. He was there when the man identified as Felix Amerge arrived, supported by a man and woman holding him up. He had taken a bath and wore clean clothes.

"I may be able to stop this attack," Felix said. "Who's commanding the forces outside the gate, do you know?"

"You could likely do that if you looked like yourself," Mara said.

"I don't look like myself, but I still have all my faculties and my memories. If the commander is someone I know, they might believe I am who I say I am."

"General Gillenbran is commanding," Mara said.

"Excellent," Felix said. "He and I go way back. Wave a flag and let them know we want to talk."

"They'll think we want to surrender," Mara said.

"Let them think that," Felix snorted. "Tell them we won't talk to anyone but General Gillenbran."

A half-hour later, six chairs were carried through the school's gates to the place where they were to meet. They had asked the army to pull back and it had. The meeting would take place outside the walls in full view of the army laying siege to the school. The Resistance would watch from the catwalk on the outer walls. Felix walked out, accompanied by Mara and Charla. Charla was nervous at being in such a vulnerable position, but she felt she needed to establish herself as the new Watcher on this world.

Of the six chairs, three faced the school, and three faced in the army's direction. Felix, Mara, and Charla sat in the chairs facing away from the school, leaving the other three chairs for General Gillenbran and his chosen officers.

"Hello Gilli," Felix said after the General and his officers sat down.

"What's going on here?" the General snarled. "Who are you?"

"They said you wouldn't recognize me," Felix said.

"And who exactly do you claim to be?" the General asked.

"Don't you recognize me? I had a place of honor at your wedding."

"Only in your dreams."

"Your oldest son was named after me."

"What nonsense is this? Felix Amerge is dead."

"You're sure about that? Take a closer look. I'm told my nose still looks like it did. It is a very distinctive nose."

The General started to protest and then stopped and stared at Felix, who continued speaking.

"I'm the man who got you too drunk to perform your marital duty on your wedding night. I held your firstborn in my arms and promised to take care of her if the day came when you couldn't."

"I don't believe it," the General said. "What happened to you?"

"Grek had me in the basement of the palace. I won't tell you everything he did. But it was bad. Very, very bad."

"It must have been," the General said.

"Can I count on your support?"

"Of course, but you'll have a hard time convincing anyone else that you are who you say you are."

"Will you speak for me?"

The General paused, then nodded his head. He stood and bowed at the waist. The two officers with him stood as well. They seemed unsure of what to do but then followed his lead. They, too, bowed and pledged their support. Behind them, the army broke their silence as they wondered what in the world had just happened.

"Who are these others with you?" The General asked.

"You know as well as I do who this woman on my right is," Felix said, indicating Mara. "But let me formally introduce you. This is Mara Morkin, the leader of the Resistance. The young woman on my left is Mellish's new Watcher, Charla." He turned to Charla and smiled. "I'm sorry I don't know your last name.

"Seastone," Charla said.

"Grek is not going to like that is someone claiming to be a new Watcher," the General said.

"You haven't heard the news yet then?" Charla asked. "Grek is dead."

"You're sure about that?"

"I saw him die with my own eyes. He died when we rescued Mara and the Prime Minister."

"Why are we still out here doing battle then? Someone should have let us know."

"I suspect that Pele has decided to take over from Grek and be the exalted leader," Felix said. "He always was ambitious."

"Of course, you're right," the General said. "Pele needs to be stopped. He'd be a terrible leader. One of the first things he'd do is get rid of anyone with the power to stop him. People like you and me."

"I agree. We need to stop him."

"Any ideas on how to do that?" The General asked.

"Plenty, starting with you letting people know that Grek is dead, and I'm still alive."

"That's a good start. Do you have any suggestions on how to do that?"

"Apparently, the Resistance does." Felix nodded toward the Resistance leader. "Mara, could you please explain your plan to us."

"We have with us a young man who once worked at the broadcast center to produce the messages on the screens," Mara said. "He quit when Grek came to power. All we have to do is get him in the building with people that the populace will trust and listen to."

"Normally, I would say that was our Prime Minister here, but since Felix doesn't look like himself, it might be hard to get anyone to believe that he is who he says he is."

"That's true, General, but people also know who you are and they trust you."

"I worked hard to win their trust. I've committed myself to speak truth. This is why it has been hard for me to see Grek in power. I supported him at first but soon realized that almost everything he said was a lie. I tried to talk to him, but the result was a demotion in rank."

"Does that mean you're not the supreme commander of the military anymore?" Felix asked.

"No, Pele is."

"We have the man who can program the equipment, but we need you to go before the people to tell them the truth." Mara held the General's eyes with her own. "Are you willing to be that man?"

"Does the programmer know how dangerous it will be?"

"He does."

"Then, the two of us will risk our lives. I can't think of a more noble cause to die for than sweeping away lies and telling the people of Mellish the truth. Perhaps I can win back my self-respect."

"Your name will be in our history books as the hero who saved our world from tyranny."

"I doubt that, but I'm still glad to do my part," the General said. "When do we leave?"

"In the time between moons, when it is dark," Felix said. "We will be flying there on dragonwing."

"Dragons! And what do you mean we?" asked the General. "You look like a slight wind would blow you over."

"Nevertheless, people need to hear from me once you establish my identity."

"I learned long ago that there is no point in arguing with you, Felix. I will be ready to leave when you are. How many of my soldiers should I take with us?"

"None," Charla said, speaking for the first time. "We only have two dragons, and it is best if they only carry three people each. Besides you two, we will take Brent, Mara, and two off-world Chosen who have special gifts."

"You're saying I can't take any of my soldiers with me?" The General did not like what he had heard.

"I have selected those who will go with you very carefully and believe they have the best chance of success," Charla said.

The General sat for a moment and stared at the new Watcher in silence. Then he nodded his head and stood up. "I'll come knocking on your gate before the first moon goes down, but if you have no objection, I'll send some of my soldiers into the city for backup."

33. The Message

The first moon was rapidly going down when Ben and Zara lifted off from Truehaven. They had an hour before the second moon rose. It was brighter than the first one, and Ben hoped they could fly fast enough to get to the broadcast station before it rose. On his back, he carried Brent, Trevor, and Felix. Zara carried the General, Mara, and Jared.

The media station was between the park and the palace. Ben was sure there would be human guards as well as drones.

They landed in a back alley. The second moon had started its climb into the sky. Once everyone had slid off his back, Ben flew up and landed on top of the roof where he could look down on the front door. Two guards were standing in front of the building.

The rising moon illuminated the street when the others stepped out of the alley. Several drones rose into the air and flew toward them.

The General shot the nearest drone out of the sky. "We can't allow them to see our eyes, and I'm not kissing anyone. I'm sure there's been a special alert put in the system for Felix. If his eyes get scanned, then every soldier in the city will immediately be heading here. Pele will bomb the station if there is any question that it has fallen into the hands of his enemies."

The guards on the media center's doorstep took out their guns and searched for targets when Ben spread his wings and dropped off the roof. He grabbed the arms holding the guns and shook them until the weapons fell to the ground.

Trevor, Zara, and Jared called on their wizard gifts to knock the drones out of the sky. Mara and the General shot them out of the air with their weapons. Drones from up and down the street flew in their direction.

Ben was still holding the guards when the others made their run for the door. "Check their pockets for a key," he said to Jared.

Jared found a key, and they quickly opened the door. Trevor used his super strength to pick both men up and carry them into the building as Ben could not enter as a dragon.

Ben stood outside the door for a moment listening to the sound of drones coming toward them from every direction. Several battle drones sporting their red lights were converging on the station. He wondered how long it would take for a human to notice there was something unusual happening here. He went into the building and closed the door before the drones arrived. Trevor had tied the men up, and he put them in front of the door to make it harder to open. The drones would wait outside the building unless something unusual happened to call them away.

The media station occupied the whole second floor. The ground level had an assortment of government offices that were closed for the night. Trevor busted open the office doors so they could make sure the building was secure. They needn't have worried. The windows all had bars on them. There was a back door to the building, but a bar across it meant it could only be opened from the inside. After making sure the ground level was secure, Jared and Trevor followed the others upstairs.

When they got to the second floor of the two-story building, they discovered a landing in front of a big heavy door. General Gillenbran knocked, but no one answered.

Mara nodded her head to Trevor, who came forward and used his super strength to kick the door open. Inside were two men and a woman. One of the men was an armed guard who stood facing the door. He shot at the intruders. The blast just missed Mara and tore out a chunk of the wall behind her. Before he could fire again, a shot from the General's weapon hit him. The man flew backward into some equipment and lay on the ground with a hole in his chest.

"General," Brent said. "We need this equipment to be operational."

"Yes, indeed," the General said and put his gun away.

On the screen in front of them was Commander Pele. The man sitting in front of the monitor sat there in shock, staring at them for a moment, then he quickly turned and moved his finger toward an icon on the screen with the word 'finished' on it. Brent pulled his chair away before he could touch it. He was about to jump out of his chair to reach it when Brent grabbed the back of his shirt and pulled him back down.

Trevor secured the man's wrists and ankles and put him on the floor.

Brent turned to the woman still sitting at the console. She made no move toward the buttons in front of her. "Are you going to help me, or do you want to join your friend."

"That depends on what you're doing," the woman said.

"We're telling the world Grek is dead."

"That's what we were doing tonight," the woman said. "In the morning, our first message was going to let everyone know Grek is dead and that he appointed Pele to take over as leader before he died."

"We are also going to tell people that Felix is alive. He was rescued last night from the dungeon in the palace."

"You're sure about that?"

"He's sure," Felix said.

The woman turned and stared at Felix. "I'll help you," she said with some uncertainty.

"Hey everyone," Brent said. "This is my friend Cortina. We used to work together."

Cortina nodded at everyone, then turned her back on them to face the screen. She hit a button, and the image in front of her disappeared.

Brent picked up a camera and took a picture of Felix. "I'm sending you a file," he said to Cortina. "I want you to superimpose a past picture of Felix over this one. I want it to slowly fade away so people can see it is the same man whose features have been drastically altered by what he experienced. While you do that, I will do a recording with General Gillenbran." Brent turned to the General and handed him a piece of paper. "This is what I suggest you say; however, you can change it if you like, but you need to keep it under three minutes."

The General took a moment to read the paper. He then handed it back to Brent. "Looks good to me."

The cameras started to roll, and the General spoke. "People of Mellish. You know me. I hope you know that I am a man whose word can be trusted. This morning I was astonished to learn that Prime Minister Felix Amerge is alive, but he is not well because he has spent the last three years in a prison cell enduring torture that we can't begin to imagine. He was rescued last night by the Resistance, which brought him to me. He has suffered a great deal but is now on the road to recovery. My soldiers and I have dedicated ourselves to seeing him continue to serve as our Prime minister."

That much had been on Brent's script, but General Gillenbran kept speaking. "In the past, we overcame our differences and learned to walk together so we could build a world where every life mattered. We never fully achieved the goal of equality, but we were on the path that was leading us there. The leaders who took over from Felix exploited our differences and were doing a good job of turning us against one another. Do we want to go back to the days when we hated others because of the color of their skin or the way they worshipped God? Do we want a world where a select few hold power and create laws to keep the rest in poverty while accumulating wealth for themselves? I say no. Join me in saying no and let us take back our world. In a moment, you are going to see and hear from Felix. He won't look like himself, but as his best friend, I can verify that it is him."

Brent nodded his head. "Great job. Now could someone please help the Prime Minister over?"

Ben and Trevor each took one of Felix's arms and helped him to the chair where the recording would happen. Brent handed him a suggested outline of what he was to say. The Prime Minister didn't even glance at it.

"I want to start by thanking those who rescued me," he said. "A healer from Earth repaired much of the damage done to my body. It will take time to restore the rest. In the meantime, I am returning General Gillenbran to his position as head of the armed forces, and I'm appointing Mara Morkin as my special advisor. Most of you will know that she has been leading the Resistance. Thanks to her efforts and the efforts of others, I am a free man. Mara is going to help me heal the divisions Grek created between the great people of Mellish. We were meant to be one people. The other good news I want to share is that Mellish has a new Watcher. The Watcher's name is Charla Seastone. She and I will be working very closely together to restore our world to the path the Guardian intends for us. Together with you, we will work for a world where peace is every child's birthright, and all our citizens experience the freedom and joy that justice brings."

The sun had risen, and the light was coming through the windows when the message they were working on was finally complete. They decided the best time to play it would be when people traveled to their workplace or had breakfast. Very few people had private vehicles, and the video played on the people movers, the sides of buildings, and in people's homes. Few people would miss the clip, whether they were at home or out on the street. The plan was to have it play over and over again until it was manually stopped. By then, almost everyone would have seen it or heard it. Although Brent thought they would be lucky if it played through from beginning to end three or four times before Pele bombed the communications center.

The people in the studio watched in awe as what they created ran for the first time. General Gillenbran spoke first. Then they had Felix speak. They started with his face from the time before imprisonment and slowly replaced it with his haunted wounded face. It was very effective, and Ben thought it was also convincing. People could see that the bone structure, the nose, and the eyes were the same, even if the face itself was drastically changed. The video clip ended with him introducing Mara, who, in turn, told the world that the restored Prime Minister had her full support.

Cortina laid her hand on Felix's shoulder. "I wasn't completely convinced you were the Prime Minister until we put this video together. I went along with it because I trusted Brent to do what is right."

"Good to know," Felix said, looking at Brent.

"We need to get out of here," Brent said. "This building will be bombed soon."

"Please, don't leave me here," the man they'd tied up begged.

Trevor cut the ties that bound his legs before they left. On the ground floor, they pulled the two guards away from the door and cut the ties that bound their legs as well.

The message was playing on the screens attached to the sides of nearby buildings. From where they were, they could see four screens all playing the same message. Every screen throughout the world was playing it. People had stopped walking and were staring. Their behavior was unusual enough that they had attracted drones who were scanning their eyes. There were no longer any at the door of the media center.

"What are we going to do now?" Trevor asked.

"It's time to go to the palace," Felix said. "There's a squatter I need to evict."

General Gillenbran led them down the street and around a corner. A soldier was waiting for them near an open-topped military transport vehicle. Felix took the seat next to the driver while the rest found seats in the back. All eyes were drawn to them as few passenger vehicles traveled the streets of Mellish.

"Look," a voice cried out. "It's him. It's Felix."

They drove slowly down the street, and the crowd following behind got larger and larger. There were thousands of people with them when they reached the palace where General Gillenbran's soldiers had arrived and were waiting for them. They were facing a higher number of soldiers under the command of General Pele.

The courtyard was also full of citizens who had seen the video and had come to support or oppose Felix's restoration as Prime Minister. When the nearby citizens saw who it was that had just arrived, most of them started chanting. "Felix, Felix, Felix."

Felix stood and waved. He then had the driver take him to the open place between the two armies. He faced the army under General Pele's command as he spoke. "I invite you to join me as we restore the rule of law to our country. I believe that everyone has the right to be treated with justice regardless of their race or religion. Are you with me? Or do we need to have a useless war that will hurt us all?"

There was silence for several minutes, and then one brave woman left the line of soldiers supporting Pele and walked over to where General Gillenbran's soldiers were. A moment later, another woman and a man joined her. Then ten more soldiers walked over. Soon there was a steady stream of people who crossed the line to join the other army. Less than thirty percent of the soldiers remained standing before the palace. They did not join General Gillenbran's troops, but they walked to the side, so they were no longer blocking his way.

Felix walked to the front door and found it locked. He knocked, but there was no answer. He nodded to Trevor, who backed up and took a run at the door, kicking it hard when he got there. The door sprang open. There was a blast of weapons fire from inside, targeting anyone coming through the open door. General Gillenbran sent soldiers wearing heavy protective gear into the palace.

"What do you think?" Trevor asked Ben.

"Let's do it," Ben said.

Ben transformed into a dragon, and Trevor climbed onto his back. Jared didn't ask if he could join them. He just climbed on. Instead of facing forward behind Trevor, he faced backward. Ben leapt into the air and flew to the dome at the top of the building. He pulled aside one of the tarps covering the space where the glass had been broken and dropped inside. There were a few soldiers standing guard on the fourth floor. They quickly disabled them and moved down to the next floor.

The soldiers on the first and second floor were attacking the troops coming in through the front door, so few noticed the threat from above. They noticed when the wizard blasts and dragonfire hit them. Those not dead or severely injured fled down the hallway. Some escaped through the kitchen door only to be captured by Gillenbran's soldiers. The battle was soon over, and Felix, General Gillenbran, and Mara entered the building.

"Where is General Pele," Gillenbran asked one of the captured soldiers.

"He's in the military command center," the soldier said.

General Gillenbran led the way, accompanied by several of his soldiers. There was a brief battle, and General Pele surrendered.

34. A New Beginning

At Truehaven, Charla spent the day getting to know the Chosen she would be responsible for training. There were only eighteen left. Many had died over the past three years as they sought to resist the rogue Watcher. Others had supported Grek in his rebellion and were not welcome to come back.

The day ended with a feast honoring several people for their role in restoring peace and justice. A similar celebration was happening at the palace. The Prime Minister requested that Mara attend to be officially named as a special advisor to the Prime Minister. Brent was named Minister of Communications. Selina was put in charge of Palace Affairs. Mort, who was now no longer just a fake boyfriend, but a real one, was given a role in the administration.

Charla recognized everyone who had struggled to restore justice and peace to Mellish. She had special words of thanks for Ben.

"My friend Ben," she said, "never gives up. If he fails, he picks himself up and rejoins the battle. When I knew Ben would be here with us, I knew everything would turn out all right. Every time I thought of him, I knew I couldn't give up, that I had to keep trying to get the Medallion.

Whenever I'm around Ben, I'm reminded that you don't have to be perfect to be useful to the Guardian."

Ben laughed. That last line was typical Charla. You never knew whether to be honored or offended by what she said. However, the truth was he wanted to be perfect, and he wasn't. He wanted to be the best at everything, but the best he could manage was being good at some things. It was hard for him to just be a cog in the wheel; he wanted to be the whole wheel or at least the most essential part. He realized that there was nothing wrong with wanting to be the best, but sometimes the only way to solve a problem was to be a team member, no more or less important than anyone else.

As he stood among the others, he thought about what they accomplished. He felt a deep sense of gratitude at being selected to come to Mellish and join the battle with such amazing people. As he stood there thinking these thoughts, Ben had a pleasant surprise. He didn't know how he knew. He just did. He was through the Wrathborn season. He was filled with joy and laughed out loud.

Later in the day, people started going home to their own worlds. Jared, Allison, Trevor, and Ben were the last to be sent through a portal.

"I hope you'll be back this way again," Charla whispered to Ben as she hugged him.

"Me too," Ben said and kissed Charla on the cheek. Charla kissed him on the lips. Ben was feeling very special until Charla hugged Jared and kissed him on the lips too.

At breakfast the next morning, Ben noticed Allison and Trevor holding hands under the table. He stared at them for a moment, wondering what was different. Then he realized what it was. There was no fire in his belly. He smiled at them before sitting beside Roku, the girl rumored to have a crush on him.

There are times in everyone's life when being able to fly high and breathe fire sounds very appealing. If you can't be a dragon, or have a dragon as a pet, then the next best thing is to write books with dragons in them and get a dog.

Dianne lives with her husband Doug, his two cats and her two dogs. When Dianne is not writing fiction or walking her dogs, she can be found sitting at her potter's wheel.